JANDIRA KAPAPELO

ANAMNESIS OF YOU

ANAMNESIS OF YOU

JANDIRA KAPAPELO

ANAMNESIS OF YOU

PENACIDADE WORDS AND WORLDS

ANAMNESIS OF YOU

ANAMNESIS OF YOU

Adults

+18

+21 ✅

TECHNICAL DATASHEET

Publisher: Penacidade Words and Worlds

Penacidade W's&W's is a fiction and nonfiction books publisher, mainly in portuguese, spanish, french, italian, romanian, german, english and dutch

Its main objective is to publish a new book every three months

Author: Jandira Kapapelo

Graduated in Management at UAL (Universidade Autónoma de Lisboa @Lisbon-Portugal)

Msc in Accounting by ISCAC (Coimbra Business School @Coimbra-Portugal) and in Marketing by ISG (Instituto Superior de Gestão @Lisbon-Portugal)

Started writing short stories as a child, when her mother used to order her to make copies, to improve handwriting and spelling errors

Published "100 Dias ao Teu Lado, 2015" with Chiado Books

Translation: Ares Jonor Etsica

Linguist, Born in Mesen (@West Flanders-Belgium)

Longtime lover of Sci-Fi, Suspense, and Drama

Lives in the city of love, Paris

Member of the Penacidade Words and Worlds team

Cover Edition: Jarres Jonor Etsica

Photographer, Born in Mesen (@West Flanders-Belgium)

Longtime lover of Romance, Fantasy, and Comedy

Lives between Waiouru, Kalgoorlie-Boulder and Singapore

Member of the Penacidade Words and Worlds team

Penacidade Words and Worlds:

.

WHATSAPP
https://wa.me/c/351910366769

TUMBLR
http://penacidade-words-and-worlds.tumblr.com

ABOOKATIME
>https://instagram.com/ABOOKATIME
>https://fb.com/ABOOKATIME/photos

BOOKSHOP
>https://bookshop.org/shop/penacidade-words-and-worlds
>https://uk.bookshop.org/shop/penacidade-words-and-worlds

FACEBOOK
https://fb.com/Penacidade

FEIRADIGITALEVENTOSANGOLA
https://feiradigital.eventosangola.com/store/Penacidade

FLICKR
https://flickr.com/people/penacidade-words-and-worlds

.

INSTAGRAM
https://instagram.com/penacidadeworlds

PINTEREST
https://pinterest.com/penacidadeworlds

TELEGRAM
https://t.me/penacidadeworlds

TWITTER
https://twitter.com/penacidadewords

VERO
https://vero.co/penacidadeworlds

Shops near you!! - @penacidadeworlds
https://instagram.com/s/aGlnaGxpZ2h0OjE3OTIzODY5Mjk1NjQwODMz

To see || To buy || To pick up || To screenshot shops

.

#search
a Lovely sense

Penacidade W's&W's
TEMPORADA || SAISON || SEASON || STAFFEL
4

9

ANAMNESIS OF YOU

TABLE OF CONTENTS

ANAMNESIS OF YOU

DEDICATION

To my father.

ANAMNESIS OF YOU

JANDIRA KAPAPELO

Joana

Joana was sitting on a bench in the street, with her test in her hand. Couldn't believe she had tested positive.

She had the perfect life. At just twenty-seven years old, she had already obtained a doctorate in economics and was working as a finance officer in one of the best companies in the country.

3

How did that happen? Why was she getting involved with a total stranger, without being careful to at least use a condom? As an intelligent woman, what was it like for her to fall into one of the worst traps the world can throw?

Joana didn't know what to think, or how to contain the pain in her heart, nor the tears that kept coming out.

How did that handsome man do that to her? He looked like the perfect man, it was unbelievable that he would transmit this great evil to her.

6

Joana thought about how she would be able to face people. They would call her a whore, a worthless woman who sleeps with anyone. Especially her father, who always raised his children to marry virgins. But, by chance, one is drugged and has already been removed from the family and now Joana who had the worst disease of all. It seems that the only saint is really Camila, Joana's younger sister, and, ironically, they never got along.

Camila, the saint who only likes to criticize people. What will happen when she finds out? And still the look of disappointment from the mother.

When she thought of her mother, Joana was even more distressed.

9

Joana took off her black boots and placed them over the bench on which she sat. It was freezing cold, but even so, she was only in her stockings. She took off her red overcoat, leaving only a shirt and black nappa pants. She opened her suitcase and took out a notebook, she was ready to end her life.

Joana would rather die than face her family. She didn't want to have to live alone forever. Without anyone, because everyone would be afraid of her.

She also removed a blue elastic and tied her straight brown hair. She picked up a pen and wondered what she could write, but nothing came to her mind. How would she explain to people the reason for her suicide? Should she lie? Should she speak the truth?

At that moment, Joana was too confused to decide anything.

12

She put aside the paper and pen she had in her hands and began to cry again. And, barefoot, she got up and started walking, from Avenida to Terreiro do Paço. She looked at the river and it was the quickest way to end her life. There was no one, it was the right opportunity.

As she approached, her heart ached even more, she couldn't think, she was afraid to die. She was afraid of dying but she was also afraid of living. She took a small step, but she couldn't. She gave a huge scream, in an attempt to calm her heart and mind, and sat up crying, for not being able to end her life. She couldn't even do that. Just one more step and it would all be over, just one more step and the pain would disappear, but Joana couldn't and that made her even more frustrated.

Her heart ached so much that, at that moment, she just wanted the presence of someone she knew. Her mom, her dad, someone who could give her a hug and say it's okay. That it wasn't the end of the world.

But the street was icy, and without a single person passing by.

15

Joana, trembling, began to walk towards her house. Barefoot and without a coat and without a suitcase. She let herself go anyway. At that moment it seemed that the cold didn't affect her.

She arrived at the house and remembered that she didn't have her keys, and that it was impossible, at least at that hour, for her to enter. She returned once more to the Avenue in search of her suitcase which, luckily, she found. And it looked intact. She decided to just take it, leaving her coat and boots behind.

Days later Joana was radiant. She had just been promoted and decided to go out with her best friend Marta.

18

Joana had just dyed her hair brown, so she wouldn't always have it black, and her blue eyes seemed less dark, but that didn't bother her. She put on a black dress that marked her curves and showed off her legs, which looked like a great actress, Rossana Ferreira. With her hair down, which made her even more beautiful.

Marta has always been a copy of Joana. They always said they were sisters, but born to different mothers, as their faces were identical. Only the eyes were different, as Marta had brown eyes. But the bodies and hair were identical.

Marta also put on a dress that left her curves well marked and showed off her beautiful legs. Unlike her friend, she always remained brunette, with black hair like an Indian's, making her look a little different from Joana.

They went to the disco bar and ordered drinks, they were willing to drink. Get drunk until you can't anymore.

21

- My God! A hottie is looking at me.- Marta says, straightening her hair and trying to seduce the strange man, making sexy gestures with her tongue.

Joana turns to see who it was and couldn't hide her smile, as she also found him very cute. He looked like someone who had just left work and gone straight to the disco to relax. He had quite long hair and wore a ponytail, the suit was very thin, he looked like a wealthy businessman, especially from the Rolex he wore on his left wrist. He seemed distracted with the iPhone 6, implying he was talking to someone important.

- It's really beautiful.- Joana replies to her friend.

- I'll go there.- Marta says, pulling her dress up, making it even shorter. She pulled her chest out, making it more visible. She went towards him, while Joana followed her with her eyes and a smile on her face.

When Joana turns around, she sees a man sitting in front of her, with beautiful black eyes. They seemed to mesmerize her, they were so big and dark, making a huge reflection with their black hair, which made him extremely handsome, even more so because he seemed to have the athletic build of a basketball player.

The black shirt and pants, also black, made him even sexier.

- Looks like your friend already won the night.- He says smiling. It seemed impossible, but Joana was a little excited by the smile of that stranger, with an accent that sounded Italian.

- It seems so.- Joana replies, also smiling, trying to hide her nervousness.

- I'm Martino.- He says, putting his lips to Joana's ear, making her shiver even more.

- Joana.- He answers, trying to lean back. Martino approaches Joana once more, as the music was extremely loud.

- Do you want to dance?

- Of course!- Joana accepts, excited.

24

Joana and Martino danced together for hours on end. They even looked like a pair of lovers, so close together they danced, appearing to be very intimate, until Martino came forward and kissed her. It wasn't like Joana, right from the first dance, to let herself be stolen a kiss, but Joana was totally mesmerized by him and was able to go to bed with him, at that moment.

- Why don't we talk outside?- Martino asks, grabbing Joana's hand and leading her out of the disco.

They walked hand in hand to Martino's car, who opened the door for her to get in. Without a single hesitation, she went in, and then Martino came in too and settled in beside her.

- Do you want to go to a specific place where we can talk?- Martino asks.

- I have nothing on my mind.- Joana replies, fascinated by that beautiful man, who looked like a gift.

- Then we can talk right here.- Martino says.

- Of course! - Joana says, looking fascinated at Martino's eyes, who, without saying anything, kissed her once more, while his hand travels over her body, making her more and more excited.

- The police might show up.- Martino mutters.

- Of course.- Joana agrees, a little disappointed and trying to compose herself.

- I have the perfect place.- Martino says. Without thinking twice, Joana agreed and they went to a hotel.

27

Martino opened the bedroom door for Joana to enter. Martino took off his shirt, standing bare-chested. Joana took a good look at the man's face. Martino grabbed her and once again kissed her, leading her to the bed. Joana opened her legs, which brought the contact even closer as he kissed her. Martino put his hand under Joana's dress, and began to caress her clit, making her even more excited. Then he penetrated her with his finger, causing Joana to cry out in pleasure in his ear, making Martino

21

also excited. Joana could feel his erect penis on her thigh, which made her even more excited. Slowly, Martino was kissing every corner of her body until he reached her wet clit.

His wet tongue made Joana even wetter, gripping the bed sheets tightly, trying to control herself, but it seemed impossible. Pleasure spoke louder.

- Put it on now.- Joana says in a husky, low voice. Martino was just waiting for that opportunity. Without a single hesitation, Martino entered her.

Joana got up from the bed, sweaty and scared, with tears in her eyes. She couldn't contain herself and started to cry once more. It seems her mind also wanted to punish her, why did she have to dream about him? Why? Will she ever be able to forget the face of that handsome young man who condemned her to a world of failure and loneliness?

Joana was startled by the noise of the telephone.

- Hello?- Answers the phone lying on the bed, with eyes still closed and not seeing who is calling.

- Good afternoon, this is Sónia Brandão, from the Santa Maria hospital. We would like to invite you to participate in group meetings, as you are likely to be in a difficult situation, so we would like to be able to help.

- I am not interested.

- Wait! Do not turn off. We have some antiretrovirals that you need to take, because she needs to start her treatment as soon as possible, and we...- Without letting the nurse finish talking, Joana hangs up her cell phone, and goes back to sleep.

30

Joana went to the supermarket, with badly cut hair, polka-dotted pajamas, slippers and her face smeared with smudged make-up because of her tears. She withdrew a huge amount of alcoholic beverages, spending 200 euros on vodka, whiskey and tequila and, without caring what people thought or commented, Joana walked past them, without looking back.

- Hi Joana, we have a board meeting, so your vacation will have to be postponed.- Upon hearing the message from Melani, her secretary, Joana threw her cell phone aside, breaking it into pieces, took a bottle of tequila and drank it straight, finishing it in less than five minutes. As she didn't eat anything, she became too weak and ended up lying on the floor for hours, until she woke up again and had another drink, which left her passed out.

Family

Marta arrives at her friend's house with the keys Joana had given her. She opens the door and smells a strong smell of alcohol and vomit. She couldn't believe that this was Joana's house, it was all dark.

Marta turns on the lamp and sees huge amounts of empty bottles scattered everywhere.

Worried, Marta takes off her coat and puts it over the armchair, starting to call out her friend's name, but without much success, as Joana doesn't respond.

3

Marta goes towards the kitchen and finds Joana stretched out in the hallway. She approaches her friend, kneeling down and putting her head in her lap, trying to wake her up but without success, no reaction. She looked dead. Desperate, Marta calls 112 and, while she waits, tries to revive her friend at any cost, but she can't.

Paramedics arrived and examined her for a few seconds, immediately placing her on the stretcher.

- What does she have?- Marta asks, distressed.

-She's in an alcoholic coma.

Martha was stunned. Joana had never been a drinker, much less to the point of falling into an alcoholic coma. And all through the ambulance ride she looked at her friend but still she didn't believe it. What happened to her?

6

Once at the Hospital, and after some time, the nurse allowed Marta to enter the room because Joana was already recovering, little by little.

Marta looked at Joana. Thank God she was fine now. The doctors said that she would be sleeping for a few hours, but that, for sure, she would wake up that day.

Joana was sitting in a cafe, wearing a skirt that made her ass look bigger, a white blouse, a blazer and black ankle boots.

9

Sitting down with a hot cup of tea. It was freezing cold, but she needed to look good for that date. Straight and silky hair thanks to the flat iron and the oil that you used before. She put some powder on her face and red lipstick, so it wouldn't look like she'd spent hours getting ready.

Joana smiled when she saw Martino from afar. He looked like a model of so much style he had. A black blazer, a white shirt underneath, a pair of jeans and brown shoes. She even hinted that the two of them had matched their robes as they were so identical.

Martino kissed her on the mouth and then sat up.

-I think we agreed!-He says, smiling at Joana.

- That's what I thought.- Joana agrees.

- Have you been here a long time?- Martino asks, with concern.

- No. I arrived just now. I ordered some tea to warm up a little.- Says Joana, who had arrived thirty minutes before the time they had agreed, plus the minutes Martino was late.

12

They stayed only ten minutes in the café, and then Martino suggested they go to the Campo Pequeno Cinema.

- I had never been to this cinema.- Joana says.

- I like this one because it is frequented by few people and we can go to one of the VIP rooms.- Martino says.

Cinema was really interesting. For just 15 euros they could eat all they wanted, and the best part was that they were the only ones in the huge, dark room with very comfortable chairs.

Joana watched Martino who seemed to be very interested in the film, while she just wanted to get out of there.

Martino placed his hand on Joana's legs, moving up little by little, until he reached her panties, which were already starting to get wet.

- What are you doing?- Joana asks, a little scared. Martino turns to her and gives her a kiss, moving his mouth up to her ear.

- Do you know why I chose to come here?- He asks, speaking and licking her neck.

- No.- Joana replies.

- If the movie didn't interest us, we would do something better.- Martino says, pulling up Joana's skirt and putting his hand inside her panties.

- Wait...- Joana asks, holding Martino's hand.

- Don't worry, nobody will show up.

15

Joana wakes up distressed, as if someone was squeezing her neck.

She was sweaty and her hand on her heart. Breathing deeply and scared.

- Calm down.- Marta says, giving Joana a hug, who looked panicked. - Calm down, I'm here. What happened?

- My life is over, all my dreams, all my goals, everything. No one will want to stay by my side anymore and I know that even my family will abandon me.- Joana says, crying, while Marta tries to wipe her tears away.

- Calm down, tell me what happened.- Marta asks, looking Joana in the eyes.

- I have AIDS.- Joana confesses.

Marta stood still, unable to speak for some time. She couldn't think of anything. His heart beat non-stop and she looked at Joana with a confused face.

- Aren't you going to say anything?- Joana asks.

- Sorry, but I don't know what to say...

- If you're like that, imagine me! - Joana says, trying to contain herself not to cry.

- I need to get some air.- Marta says, getting up from the bed and walking towards the door. When she opens it, she is startled to see a man at the entrance.

- Sorry, I didn't mean to scare you.- Says the said man, who was the doctor.

- Caro, it doesn't matter.- Marta replies awkwardly, leaving without looking back and leaving Joana even more distressed, since her best friend's reaction was not the best.

- Hello Joanna.

Joana looks at the doctor and smiles, since he's the one who gave her the bad news that she was sick.

- Hello.- She greets Joana, wiping her face.

- You look bad.- He says.

- How did you want me to be? Have you ever had HIV in your life? Look at you, you must be fifty years old and clean! I see you are married, and surely you must have children! I won't be able to have children anymore! I won't be able to get married! And you just now saw a girl leaving this room scared! Do you know why!? Because she's afraid of me, because I told her that I have AIDS and, of course, she will never want to touch me again...

- Or maybe you're just in shock and at any moment she's going to come in and give you a hug. I may never have AIDS, but I had to take care of my nephew who had it. His parents died and I had to take care of him, so I know very well what it's like to have AIDS and you can have children. You can marry. Just don't give up on living.- Joana smiles as she sheds another tear.

- What do you think?! Do you think that when I talk to a guy and tell him I have AIDS, he'll say it's okay, we can have sex with condoms for the rest of our lives, that I don't care!?!! Do you think it's that easy?!

- No. I know that is not. That's why you need to live with people who also have the same problem as you. That way they will help you get through it. Here at the hospital there is a counseling group that would certainly be of great help.

- I'm not interested!- Joana says.

- Then at least start doing the treatment, which is very important.

- Who said I want to do?

- I know that yes, I know that you caught the virus with someone you trusted and right now you may be angry. But what caught my attention is that you despaired, you cried, and I see now that during that time you got drunk and even cut your hair. You are not a bad person. If it were, she could be in clubs, angry and trying to infect as many people as possible. You can call me Gonçalo. I'm a doctor in this hospital.- Gonçalo took a piece of paper out of his pocket and placed it on Joana's desk.

- Here is the address and contact of the person responsible for the support group. One day appear!

16

Gonçalo got up and headed for the door. Before he closed it, he looked at Joana, head down wiping the tears that didn't stop falling.

- Good luck.- He said it, turning to Joana.

Joana and Martino were hugging in the bathtub. It was the first time Joana had invited a boy to her new apartment, let alone her bathtub.

- Tell me a bit about you! We went out two months ago and we never talked much.- Asks Joana.

- What do you want to know?

- I do not know. Let me start. My father is a pastor, very religious, he thinks we should only have sex after we're married.- Hearing this, Martino smiles. It was something he had never thought to hear in the 21st century.

- So, if he shows up here now...- Martino jokes.

~We're done!~Joana completes.~ My sister is the perfect daughter, always at church, she never brought problems at home. She is the pride of the family. My brother is the bad boy, I haven't seen him for over a year, we only talk sometimes on Facebook. He and my father don't get along very well, I'm... How can I explain? Half nice, half mean, my father always blamed my brother for my bad behavior. Basically, this is the summary of my family life. And thou? How is your family?

~ I am the youngest in a family of five children. Four girls and me. My father was very fond of Italy, so we all grew up there.

~ Now the accent is explained.~ Joana says.

~ But my father got a big job offer, so the whole family moved here, but today I don't feel like talking about my family. How about we do something else?~ Suggests Martino in Joana's ear.

His hand cupped her breasts. Caressing them while he placed kisses around her neck. The other hand caressed her vagina and later penetrated it, making Joana more excited. She turned and climbed on top of Martino, placing his penis inside her vagina, making gentle movements from top to bottom.

With Joana on his lap, Martino gets up and goes to the bed, where he lays her down, getting on top of Joana and, with faster and more aggressive movements, penetrates her without stopping.

18

The doorbell rings, Joana is startled, gets up towards the door. She sees that it is Martha. She hadn't heard from her friend for almost three months. Joana opens the door and looks at Marta. She looks embarrassed.

~ Can I come in?~ She asks her.

~ Of course.~ Joana agrees.

Marta enters and notices that there are no longer the pile of bottles scattered around the house like the last time. Without speaking a word she sits down and stares at the television off. Joana sits next to her, also looking at nothing, not knowing what to say to her friend.

~ Excuse me.~ Marta asks, shedding a tear.

Joana looks at her friend and just observes her, without answering.

~ You needed me and I disappeared. I know I did wrong, but I couldn't believe you had this. I wanted to comfort you, but I didn't know how. This whole time I was wondering how I could help you, but I couldn't get any answers. You were suffering so much and maybe you just needed my company but I...~ Marta starts crying, and she can't say anything else.

- It doesn't matter, I'm already glad you came.- Joana says. At this moment Marta gives her a hug, apologizing to hear from her friend.
- It's all right.- Joana says.

Pills

Marta opens the curtains, as it was so dark in broad daylight.

- This is very stuffy. How about we go to the hairdresser today, your hair is horrible! - Says Marta, holding Joana's hair, which was all damaged.

- I don't feel like anything...- Joana replies.

- Miguel called me, said you don't answer the calls. They wanted to cancel the vacation, I think you'd better call them, they've been trying to talk to you for three months.

- I know. I don't think I can keep working, I don't feel like it at all.- Joana says, lying down on the armchair.

- I talked to your doctor and he said you haven't started treatment yet. I know it's hard, but you need to start, before it's too late.- Marta says, sitting next to her friend.

- I know, I was thinking about going to the hospital.

- Then it's one more reason to take care of your hair. You can't go with that hair like that, long on one side and short on the other.

Marta took her friend's hand and lifted her off the floor.

- Let's go to the hairdresser, no excuses!

3

It's been a long time since Joana didn't even leave the house or wear any of her clothes, just wearing her pajamas.

When she put her pants on she noticed she had lost a lot of weight. They were so big it didn't look like she'd ever worn them, just like her blouse and coat. The only thing she still wore were her shoes. In her heart all she wanted to do was cry. She didn't realize at what point she lost so much weight. In her head all she thought about was death.

Marta took her friend's fragile, pale hand, squeezing it and smiling, so she could calm her down, and the two of them went into the hall. To get her hair right, Joana had to cut it, and she also asked them to dye it blonde. She didn't want to go brunette, let alone her brown, as it reminded her of things she sometimes wanted to forget.

- And you also have to do your nails!- Marta exclaims.

Joana looks at her nails and sees that they are really horrible.

When they left the hairdresser, they went shopping. Joana needed some new clothes, so they went to one of her favorite stores, as it was the only place where she could find the kind of pants that defined her ass perfectly.

- My God! Friend, look at that boy over there, he can't stop looking at you!- Marta says, all excited, with a giant smile.

Joana looked back and was really looking at her. She was of average height and an athletic build. She was wearing gym clothes, which suggested that she was someone who took great care of her body. But Joana didn't want to have anyone else. She no longer had plans for a life together. After learning of the disease she gave up everything.

6

Joana turned and walked straight out of the store.

- Let's go.- Joana asked.
- But did you find it ugly?- Marta asks.
- I'm not in the mood for that.

Joana looked at the car mirror and she was pretty cute. She didn't even look like a girl with HIV. No one can tell who has and who doesn't have HIV, her face was thinner and prettier, her new haircut made her prettier and she even looked taller. Her clothes fit her very well, making her look like a model. After two months locked inside the house, after being depressed for so long, she had managed to end her drinking and leave the house, no longer wanting to disappear, thanks to Marta. I could always count on her.

It looked like Joana was on a date, but she was just picking up her pills. She arrived at the hospital's nearly empty pharmacy, where there were only three people waiting for care. Her heart beat nonstop. She couldn't help it, she was quite nervous and couldn't stop moving her body. Suddenly, she has a huge urge to leave and when she turns around she sees a boy behind her.

- Aren't you in line? - Joana, scared, panics looking at him. - Are you okay?

-Yes...- She says, turning around.

In front there was a mirror that allowed, discreetly, to see the boy who was behind him. It was pretty cool. If it was some time ago, she would certainly have talked to him, but right now she just feels shame and fear.

9

Joana tried not to look again, but she couldn't, it seems that her blue eyes invite her to look more. They were really cute, and at the same time mesmerizing.

- Next, please!- Joana was distracted looking at the dark-haired boy with clear eyes. It looked like a version of her brother Arthur, but a little cuter.

- Madam, it's your turn.- He says, leaning against Joana's ear. She, startled, approached the counter and handed over the recipe. After a moment the pharmacist hands him a bag full of pills. Hearing nothing the pharmacist was saying, she took it and left.

Nervous and trembling, she tried to open the car, without much success. And unable to breathe properly, she tried to relax before trying again. She sits on the floor, trying to calm down.

- Are you okay?- Joana looks up to see who it was and is faced with the same blue eyes that were in the pharmacy.

She got even more nervous. Her hands throbbing, she got to her feet and turned to open the car door, knocking the bag of pills out of her hand. Flustered, she tried to pick them up off the floor. The man also bent down to help, standing there looking at one of the boxes of ARVs. Joana, with tears in her eyes, looks at the man with the pill box in his hand, standing still, unable to speak.

- Here you go.- He says, holding out his hand. Joana stared at him without being able to say anything.- You don't have to be like this, it's okay, you can take them.- Slowly, Joana received the pills and put them back in the bag.

- Are you okay? If you want I can take you in my car...

- It's not necessary.- Joana answers, opening the car door and starting right away.

Like it was easy

- Yesterday, when I went to pick up my pills, I saw a boy who reminded me of Arthur. She had the same features as him, just a little cuter. I don't know why, but in a strange way he caught my attention, I wanted to look at him, but then in my head I just thought, you have HIV and you can't keep it.- Marta, who was lying on the bed next to him. Joana hugged her. She didn't know how to comfort her friend, because one way or another she was right, it's very difficult for a guy to accept going out with her knowing her current contritions.

- And the worst part is that he knows I have HIV. My pills fell out and he picked them up. He never looked at me with disgust, I just saw pity in his eyes, something that hurt me even more. I think I will only meet two types of men in my life, those who look at me with disgust and those who look at me with pity!

- Have you thought about going to the help group?- Marta asks, stroking Joana's hair.

- Of course, I think about it every day.

- Let's go tomorrow, I can go with you, so you won't have to go alone.

- I'll see, because tomorrow I have dinner with my family. Are you sleeping here with me today?

- Of course.- Marta replies, hugging Joana.

When it's for dinner at the family's house, no tight clothes, let alone short ones. Joana therefore put on black cloth pants that did not mark her legs and a white shirt that could be zipped up to the neck, an overcoat and brown boots. She also didn't wear make-up, as her dad picks on everything.

3

Upon arrival, she took a deep breath. It's been four months since she went to that house, and now she comes back with an extra burden, she needs to try to concentrate and in no way give it away that she was sick.

- Hello mom!- Joana says, giving her a hug.

When she saw her daughter, she also gave her a big hug. Her mother was the same, always with the long and wide dresses, which did not emphasize her curves, and with her hair always tied up.

~ Hello Joana.~ Says Rui, her father.

Joana turns around and also gives him a big hug.

~ Hello, dad.

Neither Camila nor Joana were happy to see each other, but even so, they had to give each other a hug, so that their parents wouldn't realize that they weren't the best of friends. All because of a boy, who ended up not being with either of them.

~ Joana, do you sleep here today?~ Asks her mother.

~ Not today mom, but on the weekend yes.

~ A friend of mine who works for us said that you are not working and that you are about to be fired.~ Camila says.

Joana looks at Camila with an angry face and clenches her teeth to try to calm down, so as not to attack her sister.

~ I'm on vacation.~ Joana says.

~ But that's not what I heard, it seems that you gave yourself to those holidays.~ Camila teases, pouring herself a glass of juice.

~ We'll talk about it later, now let's have dinner.

~ If you're really on vacation, why didn't you come to the house?~ Rui asks.

~ I went on a trip, I only came back a few days ago.

~ And you didn't bring anything for us?~ Camila asks.

~ No, I didn't.~ Joana says, trying to fake a smile.

~ Okay, now enough talking, let's pray.~ Says Rui.

Joana was irritated as usual after coming home from her parents' house. Marta was looking at her in the rearview mirror. The reason, for sure, was Camila Filipa.

~ Stop biting your nails.~ Marta says.

~ That girl! Look, one day I lose my head! And what annoys me the most is that she pretends to be a saint to everyone, while I'm the villain.

~ I know how it is, sisters are usually like that.

~ Do you think? She seduced the guy I dated and I still think she was the one who put money in my stuff so my dad would think I stole his money. My head is in chaos today, I still have those horrible dreams that never let me forget him I don't know how long I'll have to dream about him...

~ And you never saw him again?

- Where will I see him? That bastard! That's why he never took me to his house, I understand now, I bet he continues to do that to other girls. If one day I see him in front of me, I swear I'll kill him, and then I'll go to jail, that I don't care.

- Is here. Do you want me to come in with you?

- No, I'm going alone, thank you very much for the ride.

- You're welcome. I'll be back in an hour to pick you up.

6

Joana gets out of the car and rings the bell. She has passed the avenue several times, but never imagined that there was a help center for HIV-positive people there. The door opens and Joana is startled, her heart beats with curiosity, to see the type of people who frequent the center. She sees a forty-something man who greets her at the entrance. Kind. He was a normal person, he was wearing a black suit, he looked like he was getting off work. Upon entering, he sees a woman sitting on the sofa, looking to be in her fifties, sitting with another lady who appears to be about the same age. Joana was stunned to see a teenager, pretty, thin and tall, with curly hair and green eyes who looked like she was Cape Verdean, who looked to be seventeen at the most. If she asked if she too would have HIV and how she had caught this disease at such a young age.

- Hello everyone.- Say hello to Joana.

- Hello!- They all respond in chorus.

Joana sits next to the two women, continuing to look curiously at the teenager, when her heart hurts even more when she sees that she is not the only one.

Two more came in who seemed to be the same age as the other, greeting each other as if they were old friends, and talking to each other. Another man enters, looking to be in his mid-thirties, also looking like he's just gotten off work. He was also in a suit and if she saw him on the street, she would never have guessed he had HIV.

- Hello.- He says.

-Hello.- They answer, again, all in chorus.

It was a total of eight people. Joana thought there would be more, but she was happy that they were few.

- Sorry.- Joana says to the last man to have entered.

- Hi, you can call me António.- Greets him.

- Hi, I'm Joana.

- Much pleasure!

- What time does the person in charge arrive?
- Dr. Hevandrique?
- He is a doctor?
- Of course, he's a psychologist. He should be arriving by now. Speaking of him...- says António, looking towards the door, which was opening.
- Hello everyone!- Joana's mouth dropped open when she saw the long-awaited doctor Hevandrique. He was the pharmacy man. Now she understood why he hadn't panicked. He lives with HIV-positive people daily. Unable to control his nervousness, he began to move his feet. Anyone would notice that she was quite nervous. She swallowed hard, trying to hide the nervousness that was visible to everyone.
- Hi Joana, I'm glad you came.- Hevandrique says, smiling, with teeth so white they looked like they were coming out of a toothpaste ad. He was really charming, looked like a well-groomed man, and you could tell he had an athletic build, and that he spent at least two hours a day working every bit of those muscles.

Joana looked at him in amazement, wondering if he remembers, really, really, really, her.
- Hello.- Joana said.
- This is Joana, she will start coming to the group on Tuesday.
- Welcome, Joana.- They all said in chorus.
- And we have another new person, who I don't think has arrived yet, but I don't think we need to wait for him. Let's start. Today I wanted Carolina to give us her testimony.

9

Carolina was the first teenager Joana had met.
- Hi, I'm Carolina, and I'm HIV positive. I am sixteen years old and I was contaminated when I was thirteen.

I live in Barreiro and used to live in Sintra. This story moves me a lot and if I start to cry, I apologize.- She says, already trying to hold back tears.- I had a very handsome neighbor. At least I thought he was handsome. He was about forty years old and single, he didn't have a wife or children.- She takes a deep breath before continuing the story.- Once, when leaving school, he greeted me. At that moment my heart trembled. I ran to my house, I was so nervous. The next day, the same. Until, one day, I said hello too. He smiled. His teeth were so perfect and white, they reflected in his brown eyes. I stood there looking at him. As he smiled, it melted my heart. I'm Igor, he said in a soft tone that even sounded like a melody. I swear I heard birds singing when I heard him speak. I just smiled and walked away, I dreamed about him and always prayed for classes to end, so I could find him, until one day I didn't see him. I wondered if he wouldn't come over and say hello like he always did, but he didn't show up for a week. I was sad and even cried. When I saw him again, I just wanted to give him a hug, but I couldn't. He saw that I was happy to see him and he gave me a hug. I had to reciprocate since I also wanted to hug him. The next day he invited me into his house and I went. It looked like a very cozy house. I liked the decor, it looked wonderful, he sat next to me and I was quite nervous. I just remember him telling me to relax. Then he gave me a kiss, my heart almost came out of my mouth, but I had to respond, because I wanted to too. My body behaved in a strange way. I felt his hand touching my whole body and I liked that feeling. I didn't want him to stop and gave in. When I found myself, I was already lying on his bed and that's when he penetrated me. At that moment, it was the happiest day of my life, little did I know that from that day my life would turn upside down. I dated him for a year without anyone finding out. When all of a sudden he walked away and left me with two big gifts. A child and an illness. My mother found out when I was five months old and couldn't do anything, but the worst, the biggest shock was finding out that I had HIV. My mother cried non-stop and my father had a heart attack. Luckily he didn't die.- Carolina took a deep breath and wiped the tears that fell, to be able to continue with the story.- I didn't speak to my father for many months, only when my son was born did he speak to me again. Luckily, science evolves in such a way that my baby was born without the virus and is now healthy. He is four years old and, thanks to my parents, he is happy. My parents adopted him and he is, before the law, my brother. But he knows I'm his mother. I never saw Igor again, if I saw him I don't know what I'd do, maybe I'd give him a hug, maybe I'd pass as if I didn't know him or maybe I'd invite him for coffee and tell him about our son. People who know that I have the disease ask me why I am not angry with him, I say that my anger has long since passed. Of course I was a child at the time, but I also had my share of blame, and he was a very special man in my life, he gave me a beautiful son and he was the great love of my life. Of course, I don't forgive him for giving me the disease, but I would like to at least talk to him, because he must still be passing the disease on to a lot of people, and that's what's bad. I just wish he'd stop, because as he's someone I've lived so much with and learned so much from, I'd really like him to stop and regret everything. But now, talking about my life today, I'm fine, I'm studying, I want to be a stylist and, who knows, maybe one day get married.- She says, smiling, looking like a normal teenager, who doesn't carry a big burden.

Everyone clapped their hands, while Joana was amazed to look at the girl. How can she be so strong? She looked happy, while Joana tried not to burst into tears.

- Very well! Now we're going to hear from a volunteer, to tell us his story.- Hevandrique looked at Joana, to see if she could speak, but she didn't, until António spoke.

- Hello, I'm António and I'm thirty-four years old. I am married and have four beautiful, healthy daughters. I am HIV positive, but my wife still isn't, thank God. When I was twenty-two I was arrested for making a fuss and assaulting a boy. I was sentenced to five months in jail and during that time I shared my cell with a man. For the first few weeks everything was fine, until one day, on visiting day, my mother came to see me and said I would leave early. I was so happy I couldn't stop bragging to other people until my cellmate overheard. I was happily showering when I felt my head hit the wall. When I realized that man was raping me, I never thought such a thing could happen to me. When he was done, he spat on me and walked away. Deep down, he knew I wouldn't tell anyone out of shame, and I didn't. It traumatized me so much that I couldn't be with girls. I hardly ate. I tried several times to kill myself. I saw that my mother, even though she didn't know it, suffered with me, I couldn't stop thinking about it, until one day I opened up to her. She took me to a psychologist and with his help I was able to overcome this trauma. One day, when I was feeling really bad, I went to the hospital and there was nothing wrong, I had several tests and nothing. However, later I decided to take the test, it came back positive, and it was another new chapter of agony in my life. I went to the jail to look for the man, but he was already out. I wish I could talk to him, ask him why he did that to me, but they couldn't tell me where he was. I got desperate and tried to end it all, but I couldn't. My mother arrived on time. From then on, I was grateful for the wonderful parents I had, who supported me at all times. I found out that I was HIV positive when I was twenty-four and from that moment on I was already planning my life alone, as I imagine that no one would accept being with me. But luckily, when I was doing my master's, I met a nice girl, with whom I fell completely in love. Whenever I saw her my heart ached, but I could never be with her. First, I was afraid of contaminating her, and second, I didn't know if I would have the courage to tell someone that I had the disease, until, finally, one day she came to talk to me, asking us to work together. I accepted. At least I wanted to be her friend. When we were doing the work she gave me a kiss. I was so scared that I fell off my chair, leaving her scared too. I remember yelling at her, asking her not to do that anymore, and I left. I researched to see if a person could contaminate someone in the exchange of saliva, but luckily no. I was so relieved. The next day I wanted to walk past her without saying hello, but she walked right past me without even looking me in the eye. I thought it was for the best, until she met me at the subway station and asked me if I was gay. I wanted to say yes, but at that moment she didn't feel like lying, and I said no. So I'm the ugly one, she replied. That sentence left me so down that tears almost came to my eyes. I saw that she was sad, maybe because she liked me. I noticed the subway was coming and looked into her eyes, telling her I had HIV. I saw a panicked expression on her face. So much so that she didn't move. I went away and left her there, on the bench at the station. When I went to school I was filled with fear, imagining that maybe she had told everyone that I had HIV, but luckily she didn't, everyone treated me the same. I was sitting waiting for the teacher and she sat next to me. I was amazed that she still wanted to sit with me, and when class was over, she asked to speak with me. I was quite nervous, but I went with her anyway. I can stay with you anyway, I don't care, I've been researching and there are couples where one has HIV and the other doesn't, she told me. I was so happy that she agreed to stay with me, even though she knew I had a terrible disease, that I could only do one thing. Ask her to marry him. And that's what I did. We have been married for six years and have four daughters. As I said before, they are all healthy.- After António's testimony, time had run out and they had to say goodbye.

10

Joana was waiting for Marta at the door of the building. She would still take another fifteen minutes to arrive.

- Hello Joana.- She turns around and sees Hevandrique.
- Hello doctor.- She says, putting her hands in her coat pocket.
- Next week we can count on your testimony? - He asks.

Joana was a little irritated with Hevandrique. The real reason she didn't even know what it was.

- I'm not ready for this yet.- She says, looking at the floor.

- It's okay, we'll wait until you're ready.- He says with a smile, which made Joana even more irritated.

- You keep motivating people, as if the life of a person with AIDS were easy, I bet you couldn't stand a year with AIDS, you might think you know what it is but you don't. You have no idea what it's like to have to take nine pills a day, you don't know what it's like to be ashamed of every person who passes by on the street, you don't know what it's like to have to live in hiding and not be able to go out with anyone because you are infected with AIDS. So do me the favor of not talking to people with that smile, because with that you don't calm anyone, it just makes people even more angry!- Joana fires, leaving Hevandrique not knowing what to say.

Marta arrived just in time, honking her horn so that Joana would notice. Without thinking twice, Joana turns her back on Hevandrique and goes to her friend.

Hospice

Today was the day to go back to work after being at home for so long. She went to her office and was amazed at the amount of paper she found on the table. She had a lot of work to do. Joana sat down, crossing her legs and closing her eyes, in order to relax a little. Carmem, the assistant, opened the door causing Joana to open her eyes and come face to face with her. Carmem informed her that the director was waiting for her.

Joana was prepared for anything, even to be fired after being promoted.

Upon entering, she saw the director of human resources, it looked like the white hairs had grown along with his belly. It felt like, instead of a few months of absence, it had been years.

- Hello Renato!- Joana says, sitting down.

- What happened?- He asks.- We needed you. We were closing a big deal and it was necessary to have our finance company here. You are responsible, how could you do this to us?- He says, getting more and more nervous.

- I thought I was on vacation, I didn't know I should come to work, even on vacation.- Joana says, trying to contain her nervousness.

- I had told you to leave your cell phone always on.- Answers Renato, taking a deep breath.

- Sorry, I didn't think such a thing could happen.

3

Renato sat in the chair, turning his back to Joana and placing his right hand on his face. He was trying to calm down.

- After work, there will be a meeting, where we will discuss your future here at the company.- He says in a low voice. Despite this, Renato was very fond of Joana and did not want to fire her. He knew she was competent and people like her are hard to find.

- It's ok.- Joana says, getting up.- Can I go now?

- Yes.

Martino trembled while he slept, making Joana realize this and startle her. He got up and grabbed his forehead, noting that it was quite hot. He was shaking so much that she was getting worried. Joana got up and went to get a washcloth and a basin with cold water, starting to clean his face, which was quite pale and wet with sweat.

- Joana...- He said with a hoarse and trembling voice, seeming to be suffering immensely.

- I'm here.- Joana says, scared.

-Please don't leave me alone.- He asks, squeezing Joana's hand. Looking like a child afraid of the dark.

- I would never do that.- Calm him down, Joana, wiping his face with the towel.- You'll be fine. If you want, we can get a doctor tomorrow.

- No! It's just the flu. Tomorrow I'll be as good as new, just give me a hug.- Joana agreed and they fell asleep hugging each other.

Joana opened her eyes, tired, after another night of having to dream about Martino. Would she ever stop dreaming about this man? thinks Joana clutching her chest. She couldn't stand having to dream about him anymore.

- Please God, make me stop dreaming about him.- Joana said, lying down and looking at the sky.

- Time to get up!- Marta says.

- Hello mom.- Says Joana, trying to make fun of Marta.

- Your sister says she'll be here soon.

6

Joana got up awkwardly, went straight to her bedside to collect the pills, heading for the bathroom.

- What happened?- Marta asks.

-I have to keep all this, you know how that girl is, she likes to mess with everything, she even discovers my pills. If I don't contain it, nothing will stop her from telling my parents that I have HIV.

- Yes, you are right.

Marta helps Joana store the pills and, as soon as Joana puts them in the safe, Filipa slams the door. Joana opens it and looks her up and down, looking at her and noticing her long dress, which made her a true devotee, without showing any part of her body.

- What do you want? - Joana says, with a face of few friends.

- What do you mean? - Filipa says, entering without Joana inviting her in.- I came to visit my older sister. I like your new haircut, I think I'll do the same.- She says, sitting on the sofa.- What's for breakfast?- She asks, looking at every corner of the house.

- Nothing, now go away, we need to go to work, something you, even at twenty-five, never heard of.

- I'll follow in my father's footsteps, I'll be a shepherdess.- Filipa says, with an air of superiority.

- All right, now go away.

- Is that how you treat your little sister?

- Filipa, go away now!- Joana says, with a serious voice.

- It's all right. Dad wants me to come live with you. I think a month from now. They're going to Brazil for a meeting, so get ready, because we're going to share the same house.- She says smiling and then immediately kisses Joana's cheek before running to the door and closing it without sister had time to react.

As soon as Filipa leaves, Joana screams in anger.- Now, your life is going to be hell.- Marta comments.

9

Joana went to the gym. The doctor advised her to do physical exercise, to fortify the organism. She put on a black tracksuit, which Marta had given her. Joana was in a bad mood, she wasn't much for exercising, but she couldn't give up, because Marta had already signed up, knowing that exercise would be the last thing Joana would want to do.

Joana goes to the treadmill and starts to walk on it, so slowly that, in this way, she was worse than a baby crawling.

- I think you have to run more.- Says Hevandrique, to Joana's surprise, who almost fell off the treadmill with such a shock.

- What are you doing here?- Joana asks.

- I think I came to sleep, my bed is not very good, so I have a fetish for sleeping in the gym. You know, I don't know where I would have gone to learn that.- Joana looked at him, seriously.- Sorry, I was just trying to liven up our conversation.- He says, laughing at his own joke.

- It wasn't funny.- Joana says, with a face of few friends.

- I also exercise here. I also live in Saldanha. Just like you.- she clarifies, winking her left eye at Joana.

- How do you know that I live in Saldanha?

- On the day of the pharmacy, I had to follow you, to make sure you got home safely.

- And why did you do that?- Joana asks, confused and with an even more serious face.

- Because you weren't well, and...- Without letting Hevandrique finish speaking, she cut him off.

- I'm not your patient, I'm not your friend, so never do that again. I don't need compassion from people like you, because when you do those kinds of things it just makes me worse than I already am. I don't know what your goal is, but if it's to make me feel bad, you can celebrate, because you've achieved it.- Joana says, her eyes full of tears, trying to keep them from falling.

Joana returns to the treadmill and continues to walk slowly like a chameleon. Next door, Hevandrique starts to run. Somewhat annoyed, she moves to another machine, on her feet. So that she wouldn't be too close to Hevandrique.

12

Joana was annoyed, in a strange way. Hevandrique disturbed her and made her quite irritated. Maybe it was the fact that she might never get a chance to date him, so she kept him as far away as possible. As much as she liked António's story, not all healthy people are willing to be with a sick person, let alone a disease that is communicable.

- Can you give me some water? - Asks Hevandrique, standing in front of Joana, wiping the sweat with the towel.

- Why didn't you bring it?

- I even brought it, but it's over.

- Then go to the bathroom.

- You are a very difficult person...- He says, heading towards the bathroom.

- Wait!- Joana exclaims, sighing.

- Thank you very much.- He says, picking up the bottle.

- What are you doing?- Joana asks.

- I'm drinking water, isn't that what you called me for?

- But you had to at least wait for me to give you permission to drink. Wait, I have another bottle in my suitcase.

- You don't have to.- Answers Hevandrique, drinking from Joana's bottle.

- You...- Joana begins, astonished.

- What is it?- He asks.

- Anything.

- So until tomorrow, at the meeting.- He says goodbye, giving Joana a kiss on the cheek, leaving her blushing and with a slight smile.

- Hello, I would like to talk a little about my miserable life...- Cassandra speaks, between words and sobs.- I caught the virus when I received a blood transfusion, I had suffered a serious accident. My son was getting sick at school, so I went to meet him in such a hurry that I crashed into a truck. I was seriously injured and I almost died. Nobody had the same blood type as me, but luckily, a gentleman came along and donated some of his blood to me. Thanks to that, I got better, I was hospitalized for three months. On the day I was discharged, I also received the worst news of my life, I was contaminated. The doctors were so worried about saving my life that no one thought to do a test on that blood that was being donated. I told my husband, who the next day asked for a divorce and said that my children would grow up better with him than with an infected woman. I fought him in court, but I lost. Even the judge thought that an HIV positive person does not have enough autonomy to care for children. My husband received a job offer to work in Dubai, and he went with my children. I haven't seen any of them for ten years, one of these days I'll die and I won't see my children. I only talk to them on the internet, they hardly speak to me and they even call their stepmother mother. My life is like this, the last time I saw my children, one of them was 14 and the other 10. They are all grown up but none of them love me. When I call they are always busy, I never spent more than two minutes talking to any of them. I tried to rebuild my life, but the last person I hung out with left me as soon as he found out I had HIV and, on top of that, told everyone. I had to move and I was never able to return to my homeland, out of shame. For my mother I died and my father has Alzheimer's, he doesn't even remember that he has a daughter. My brothers try to say hello to me sometimes, but deep down, they're also afraid of me, and they only do it because their conscience is heavy. I've tried to put an end to it countless times, but in a strange way it feels like someone is stopping me. I ended up having to stay in an asylum for three months. I think that place was the best place I've been in my last ten years. Those people may be different, but they don't have prejudice and I felt quite good there. Every day I ask myself, why, why, why, why, why? I didn't do anything wrong, it was a medical error, why do I have to suffer so much?- She says, unable to contain herself, and started crying non-stop.

- If you want, you can stop for a while.- Says Hevandrique.

- No, I want to continue.- She answers, wiping her tears.- When I left the asylum, I thought that maybe I would meet good people, without prejudice, like those. But no, it seems like every person I meet just makes me more and more disappointed. I hope that, at least here with you, I don't feel so alone. Yesterday, both stories were so good and motivating, but today you're going to have to settle for my crappy life story. Because of this damn disease, I lost everything, I have nothing left! I depend on the State for a living, as I had to leave my old job and, to this day, I haven't been able to get a new one. I wanted so much for my life to change, for my children to talk to me again, I would like to find someone to share my life with, even if it was just a friend, because I don't even have that.

The mood in the room grew heavy. After Cassandra's deposition. No one else could say anything. Even Hevandrique was crestfallen at the woman's sad story. It was a horrible story and no one deserved to go through that. Indeed, fate had taken a heavy toll on her.

15

~ Do you want to drink some coffee?~ Hevandrique asks Joana.

~ No.

~ Come on, it's just a coffee...~ He says, trying to make a spoiled boy face.

~ I know it's just a coffee but I don't feel like it. And it's getting cold. Don't speak to me, because I'm getting cold in my mouth.

Joana observed that Hevandrique was still beside her, seeming to be waiting for someone, but Joana didn't want to ask anything, so she wouldn't have to start a conversation.

Joana sees Marta approaching, on foot.

~ So Marta, what happened to the car?

~ There's a lot of traffic, so I parked on that side.

~ Okay, so let's go.~ Joana says.

~Hello, I'm Marta!~She greets, addressing Hevandrique.

~ Nice to meet you, I'm Hevandrique, Joana's friend.

~ Really? ~ Marta says, with an enthusiastic smile.

~ No, he's just the psychologist who listens to our lamentations.~ Cut Joana.

~ It's not like that...~ Hevandrique says, putting his hand on his head.

~ I invited her, just now, for coffee, but I was automatically rejected.~ Hevandrique says, rubbing her hands, trying to warm up.

- So come on, I know a great cafe...- Without letting Marta finish speaking, Joana immediately cut the subject.

- If you want to go, you can go, but I'm sleepy and I have to work tomorrow.

18

Joana crossed the road, with Marta following her, saying goodbye to Hevandrique and leaving with her friend.

Blanket

Joana entered the house annoyed, after not speaking a single word the entire way. Marta followed her in an attempt to understand what was going on.

- What happened?- Marta asks, closing the door.

Joana sits on the sofa and leans her head against the pillows, closing her eyes. Marta also sits next to her friend.- What is it?-She asks again.

Joana sits up straight and takes off her coat.

-Don't you understand that he does it because he feels sorry for me? He's the same guy from the drugstore, and on top of that, he's in the same gym and in the same neighborhood as me.

- You like him.- Marta says with pity. Joana looks at Marta with a startled look, as if she had said the worst nonsense of all.

- Where did you get that idea from?

- I know it's complicated, that you think he's going to dump you because you're contaminated, but you don't know what his true intentions are, so if you like him, you should at least give him a chance.

- I know very well what he wants. He wants me to be like everyone else at the center too, treating him like he's a god, so he

he is being so nice to me.- Joana says, taking off her boots.

- And if he likes you, as I am now realizing that you like him?

- Where did you get that? I don't like that cocky person, besides, he's not even my type.

- That's not what you told me the first time you saw him.

- I had seen wrong! Now either stop talking about it or leave!

- You don't need to lie to me, I'm your friend.- Marta says, putting her hand over her friend's leg.

Joana looked at her friend. For a few seconds she wanted to admit yes, but then she gave up, wanted to keep it to herself. Maybe if she just kept it to herself, one day that feeling would disappear.

Martino had a high fever every night, something that was worrying Joana, but as it was freezing cold, and he also had the flu, Joana associated the fever with the flu.

- Good morning.- Joana says, enjoying Martino's face as he opens his eyes.

- Good morning.- Martino replies, giving him a kiss.

- Are you feeling better today?

- Yes.

- How about we go for a walk?- Joana asks.

- I don't feel like going out today.- Martino says, head down, lying on the bed and closing his eyes.

- Well then, I'll go for a walk alone.- Joana says, getting up from the bed.

- Wait… I'll go with you.

3

Joana went to the café to get pills, while Martino waited outside for her. When Joana returned, Martino was gone. She tried asking a few people but without much success.

He was around two hours waiting for him and nothing. He returned home and searched every corner of her apartment and nothing. She called him several times, but it went straight to voicemail. Joana was getting desperate, she didn't know his family and she didn't have the number of anyone who also knew him, where could he be?

-Hello everyone, who is going to share his story with us today?- Hevandrique asks, looking at Joana, who was returning the look with the face of few friends.

- It could be me.- Says the owner of the house.- I'm Francisco and I'm HIV positive. To this day, I still don't know the exact moment when this happened. I've always liked dating a lot. I remember that every time I had casual sex, I always used a condom, so I don't remember the day I was beaten. I was also not lucky enough to find someone who would accept me the way I am, but even so, I didn't give up. I think I can still fall in love with someone who accepts me for who I am. My family supports me, I have a twenty-year-old son, who also supports me, he does not have the virus, thank God, and he is currently in Coimbra studying medicine. His mother lives in Faro, with a new family, and I, for now, live alone since my son moved to study, but he always spends his holidays here. I go out with my friends, with my brothers, sometimes with my parents. They always support me, the only thing missing in my life is a companion. This is my little story.- Francisco ends, looking at Cassandra, smiling.

- Thank you so much for sharing your story with us.- Thanks Hevandrique.- Anyone else want to share something?

- Me.- Says one of the teenagers.- I'm Mariana, I'm eighteen years old and I have the HIV virus, just like all of you. As I was leaving school, a group of men approached me, asking for money. As I didn't have one, they threatened me with a knife and forced me to go with them without making any noise. They took me to a secluded place. I was panicking and in my head I just thought those men were going to kill me at any moment, but instead they raped me, and as a result, I got the virus. In the first few days, I didn't accept it, I refused to admit that I was infected, and when it hit me, I just wanted everyone to contract the virus. I devised a plan to meet as many people as possible and pass the virus on. My mother found my diary and luckily discovered the plan, taking me to the psychologist. It was there that I met Dr. Hevandrique. I can say that it changed my life, and now I accept what I have, and that it's not the fact that I have it that everyone should have. I will continue to do my treatment, so that the disease does not progress. I told my boyfriend what happened and luckily he supports me. He said he would never leave me for the simple fact that I was contaminated. I was even surprised, to hear something like this from such a young person.- As soon as Mariana finishes, Hevandrique gives her a hug.

- Does anyone else want to share his story with us?- Heandrique asks, but no one speaks.- So we end our meeting for today.

6

Joana and Hevandrique, as usual, stayed under the building waiting for Marta, who was already half an hour late.

- Don't you think it's better to call her?- Hevandrique asks, shivering from the cold.

- You can leave if you want.- Joana says, also shaking and rubbing her hands.

Hevandrique started walking and Joana was surprised to see him go. She always told him to go away, but she never thought he was for real. Although, when they are alone, they hardly exchange a word, but Joana enjoyed Hevandrique's company very much, even though it was a mute company.

- Are you seriously leaving?- Joana shouts. However, Hevandrique continues to walk, without looking back. - It's ok, I don't care.- Joana shoots, angrily, sitting at the door, waiting for Marta.

- I went to the other side of the street and your friend didn't show up.- Says Hevandrique. Joana was face down and couldn't show it to Hevandrique, as she was trying to hide a smile of relief that he hadn't left.

- And why did it take so long to get to the other side of the street?- Joana asks, looking at her feet.

- I went to get a blanket I have in the car. I know that if I offered you a ride you wouldn't take it, so here you go.

- I dont need. You can leave if you want.

- I think when I tried to go, you almost cried for me to stay.- Hevandrique jokes.

-You misunderstood.- Joana replies.

- Do you want me to call a taxi?

- I'm going with my friend.

- You don't have a cell phone? So why don't you call him?

Joana continued to look at her feet, not saying a single word.

Hevandrique knelt down, took Joana's face in her hands, lifting it and giving her a kiss.

- What are you doing? - Joana says, pushing him and getting up.

- Sorry.- Says Hevandrique, confused, on the floor.

- I don't know what you want from me, but I'm not willing to suffer for someone who, at any moment, can change me for a healthy person.

Joana leaves there irritated, walking as fast as possible.

- Wait, Joana!- asks Hevandrique, getting up from the floor.

Joana sees a taxi and immediately climbs in, leaving Hevandrique behind.

Against the wall

- I can't believe he kissed you!- Marta says, screaming.
- Calm down, it was just a kiss.

Marta was jumping on the bed, she was so happy, looking like a teenager who got a 20 on her test.

- For! If you break the bed, buy another one!- Joana says, trying to catch Marta to force her to stop.
- Sorry, I'm so excited! It's just that today a guy with whom I already exchanged some messages invited me to have a coffee with him. But now tell me! And after the kiss?
- I pushed him and left, I told him I'm not staying with him.
- But you like him.
- I like it so much that every night I dream about the other one.- Joana ironizes.
- I bet that when your dreams come to an end, you won't even remember his name.- Marta says, giving her friend a kiss on the forehead.
- Who knows…- Joana says, turning away.
- Are you going to sleep now?- Marta asks.
- Of course, tomorrow I have to wake up early, especially after giving me a second chance, I can't waste it.

Marta lies down beside Joana, hugging her.

- You don't even look like the girl who wanted to give up everything, I'm very proud of you, friend.- Marta says, making Joana smile.

Joana woke up to her alarm clock for the first time in months. Today was the first time she didn't dream about Martino. Joana is truly happy, it seems that her nightmares have finally come to an end. The chapter of her life that Martino was a part of now seems to have ceased to exist. Looks like she can start over now.

- Martha, wake up!
- Hhummmmm, let me sleep…- Marta grumbles.
- You'll be late.

- I bet it's still early, you usually wake up two hours earlier.- Marta says, turning to the other side.

- I know, but today I didn't dream about Martino and woke up with the alarm clock, it's already 07:00, good luck!

Marta, hearing the time, gets up and goes to the bathroom.

- No!- Joana says, blocking the door.- I woke up first, so I shower first.

- But then, I'll be late!- Marta says.

- While I take a shower, you prepare your clothes and brush your teeth.

3

Two more young men appeared in the group, in their early twenties. One of them named Thiago, who was frowning, looking like he had been forced to go to the counseling group, while Tomás, the other, had a wet dog face, looking as if he had been crying all night.

As usual, Hevandrique arrived five minutes after 10:00.

- Hello everyone!- Greets Hevandrique, while everyone makes the usual circle.- Hello Tomás and Thiago, welcome. I am Dr. Hevandrique and, as we have new participants, I would like to give my testimony, as there are people who still don't know that I am also HIV positive.- Joana looks at Hevandrique in terror. It never crossed his mind that he might also be HIV positive.

- I am thirty years old and I contracted the virus thirty years ago. My mother and father were carriers, so I was born with the virus. My mother died during childbirth and my father died when I was just five years old. Who raised me was an uncle. He was the person I considered as a father, who raised me along with his children, without ever discriminating and, above all, without any fear that I could transmit the virus to one of my cousins. One of my cousins and I are the same age, and we've been together since kindergarten. When we went to high school, we were in puberty and my uncle always told me that it was best for me not to date, at least to avoid accidents. Since I knew my situation very well, I simply obeyed.- Joana looked at Hevandrique and couldn't believe what she had heard. She looked scared. It looked like I was watching a horror movie, because of her face.- When a girl came to me and said she wanted to be my friend, I was happy as hell, as she was one of the prettiest girls at school. I just never imagined that she would fall in love with me, and my cousin with her. During a school party, she gave me a kiss. It was my first kiss, and it was ahead of everyone else. My cousin went crazy with rage and I remember he punched me. I fell to the floor and he climbed on top of me, giving me another one. My nose started to bleed. My uncle always told me not to let anyone touch my blood, so I pushed my cousin not to touch him, but that made him even angrier. He has HIV, he shouted. It was a new disease and everyone was afraid. The girl who had kissed me was crying because she was afraid, as the teachers talked about HIV as if it were the worst thing in the world. On the same day, the principal asked to call my uncle and told him that I would have to leave the school. My uncle asked me to stay only until the year was over and the director accepted. It was one of the worst experiences of my life. Nobody touched me, I was treated like a disgusting creature. When I went home, the kids threw stones at me and my uncle always had to go looking for me, because I would come home wounded. I saw that I wasn't the only one to suffer, so I had to be strong. My only wish was to get out of that school, even if it cost me a year of my life, but I couldn't ask my uncle to do that, he did so much for me that I preferred to continue to suffer in silence. Even my teachers were afraid of me, I was isolated and every day there were parents asking me to get expelled as soon as possible. I remember that, once, the girl who kissed me found me in the courtyard alone and told me that if I had infected her, she would kill me. She spoke with such hatred, I was afraid. She wasn't the only one who said she would kill me if she infected her. But her threat was so frightening, I always prayed she was okay. That she hadn't contracted the virus, because even the kids were afraid of her. Nobody spoke to her and, in a way, she suffered from it too. One day, I remember that a group of colleagues ambushed me. There were about five of them and they had sticks and stones. In that moment, I knew I could die, looking at the expressions of anger and hatred. They were actually quite angry with me, when, in desperation, I broke a bottle and slashed my wrist, threatening them with my blood. Finally, they ran and disappeared. From that day on, I never went to school again. I didn't tell my uncle anything, and every day, during school hours, I hid in a nearby forest. On the other hand, the principal did not warn my uncle, because it was already his desire that I leave there, due to all the pressure that was being made by the students' parents. Until the year ended and, of course, I failed. The good part is that I left that school. But my drama didn't stop there. When I changed schools, it seemed that the rumor that there was an HIV-positive student had spread. In the first years, they didn't know who it was, but in the 5th year they found out and, once again, my life became hell. However, at that time, knowledge about this disease had evolved a lot, and there was not as much fear as before, but even so, there was still a lot of prejudice. If it still exists today, imagine the old days. My life got better in 12th grade when I met a girl who didn't care that I was HIV positive. We dated for some time. We have always kept ourselves informed about the disease. So well informed, we were together until her father found out and sent her to college abroad. I waited three years for her. But she never came back. Then the family moved house, and I lost contact with her. I've had three perfectly healthy girlfriends since Carolina. None of them became infected. So, this is my story.- Hevandrique says, sighing.- Now, do any of the new members want to share his story?- Joana was perplexed, looking at Hevandrique, without saying a single word.

- I just want to leave.- Thiago says, nervous, wanting to get out of there.

- All right.- Says Hevandrique.

- I'm only twenty-two years old, how did this happen to me? - Tomás cried, with his head down, muttering in disbelief for having HIV.

- Stop being a sissy.- Says Thiago.

- Don't speak to me!- Tomás replies, full of anger, shooting Thiago with his eyes.

- Now it's my fault?- Provokes Thiago, smiling. Which makes Tomás leave his place and go after Thiago. The two fall to the ground and Tomás attacks Thiago with numerous punches. Hevandrique and António intervene, separating them.

- Both of them stop!- Antonio says.

-Let me go!-Screams Tomás, pushing António and taking his coat, as he leaves the room.

- He thinks it's my fault, it seems...- Says Thiago, wiping the blood from his mouth. Moments later, Thiago also takes his coat and leaves.

- It seems that today didn't go very well, so let's close our meeting, we can leave it for next Tuesday.

- Were you waiting for me?- Hevandrique asks, seeing Joana sitting on the stairs of António's house.

- Of course not.- She says, standing up.

- Then why didn't you wait outside, as usual?

- Because today is very cold.- Mind Joana.

- I just don't understand why she always arrives late.- Says Hevandrique, leaning against the door.

- She has things to do. She tell me just one thing. Why did she never tell me before?

- Tell what?- Joana looks at Hevandrique.- Oh, about the illness!?- Hevandrique exclaims.- I thought you knew. Of course, when we met at the drugstore, you had no way of knowing, but when you saw me in the group, I thought you had joined. Of course, later I noticed that no, from the things he said. I tried to give you some time to find out for yourself, but it seems like you'd never get there.

- You're calling me stupid.- Joana says indignantly.

- Of course not! What a complicated dictionary you have.- He says, smiling.

Joana pushes Hevandrique aside, annoyed, and opens the door. Hevandrique pulls her arm, placing her against the wall, pressing his face to hers. Joana starts to take a deep breath, while she waits, with an afflicted look, for Hevandrique to kiss her. - This time I won't be knocked down?- Hevandrique asks, brushing his lips against Joana's lips, and lowers them, starting to kiss her neck. Hevandrique puts his hand under Joana's blouse, caressing her back.

- What time are you going to kiss me? - Joana asks, in Hevandrique's ear. At that moment Joana's phone vibrates and Hevandrique removes his hand from her back, placing it on her head.

- Looks like it won't be today.- He says.

Marta

Joana woke up at six in the morning, on a Saturday, took a long shower, put on a tracksuit, which she had bought herself, which left her ass well defined, as well as her cleavage. She did a simple makeup and put on some perfume. She didn't want to look ugly, as she was going to find Hevandrique.

- Stop making noise!- Marta begs, covering her head with the sheets.

- You're going back to your house today.- Joana says, putting a gloss on her lips.

- What?- Marta asks, sitting on the bed, amazed.

- Today I want to be alone.- Joana replies.

- What? I can't believe you're going out with him!- Marta says excitedly.

- Perhaps. It all depends on today's meeting.- Joana says, picking up her suitcase and heading to the door.

- Good luck!- Marta still shouts.

Joana looked around and couldn't see Hevandrique. It seems that, precisely today, he decided to miss it. Whenever she arrived, he was already there, but today, to Joana's misfortune, it seems he wasn't.

- Hello!- Joana turns around, excited, hoping to be Hevandrique. Her being disappointed to see that he was just one of her gym mates. She always saw him there, as he was quite tall and had a good physique, so he didn't go unnoticed by women. But they had never spoken. I wonder what made him talk to her today? Joanna thought.

- Hello.- Joana says.

-You seem to be looking for someone... I'm Marco.- She introduces herself, smiling.

- I'm Joana, and I'm not looking for anyone.- Joana says, a little embarrassed.

- Not me? - He asks, with an air of smugness, leaving Joana gaping.

- How about we have a coffee, when we finish training?

- Sorry, next time. I already have things scheduled for today.

- Okay, so we can make an appointment for another day.- Marco replies, with a sad expression in his eyes.

- Of course.- Joana says, trying to force a smile.

- So, see you later.- Marco says goodbye, heading to the changing rooms.

3

Joana takes a deep breath and, turning around, almost falls to the side when she sees Hevandrique standing behind her, with a smile that made her melt.

- Hi...- Joana says, sighing.

- Looks like you have a date.- Hevandrique says.

- It's just Marco. He's our gym classmate, nothing important.- Joana clarifies, a little confused.

- Wow, and I wanted to ask you out, I think I'll get a no too.- Says Hevandrique, trying to make a face of a spoiled baby.

- You will only know if you invite them.- Joana says, walking towards the treadmill, with a victorious smile on her face.

- Do you have plans for tonight?- Hevandrique shouts.

- You can pick me up at 8:00 am.- Joana replies.

- I thought I told you to go away.- Joana says, with her eyes closed, while Marta did her makeup.

- If I were, who would make up for you, ungrateful?

- I don't want to see you here after 10:00.

- How selfish. I had plans to have a threesome.- Marta jokes.

- Don't make me laugh, otherwise I'll still leave here blurry.- Joana says, trying to contain her smile.

- Don't worry, I'm a professional.

The doorbell rings, making Joana nervous. She goes to the mirror and sees her makeup a little exaggerated, because of the heavy red lipstick and false eyelashes that her friend forced her to put on, in addition to the dress being a little too low-cut.

- I'm feeling like a bitch. All I needed to do was paste a eat-me on my forehead.- Joana complains.

- You look beautiful. Besides, that's what they're for.- Marta says, smiling.

- Let me go and open the door.- Joana says, looking nervously at her friend.

- Go on, don't keep the man waiting. And that you have your waxing done!-Says Marta, making Joana's heart drop to the floor by remembering that she doesn't have her hair removal in good condition. She turns and looks at her friend with a panicked face.

- I didn't shave my bikini line!

- My God!- says Marta, getting up from the bed and running towards Joana, lifting her dress and peeking under her panties.- That's not very good...

- What do I do?

- You have to pass a blade!- Suggests Marta.

- But I'm allergic to the blade.- Joana answers, worried.

- Do you have depilatory cream?

- No, I've never waxed at home.

- That's it, I have new blades here. It'll have to be a blade, or you'll get the hairy monkey.

- Okay, give it to me. Open the door and distract him for a while.

- All right.- Accedes Marta.

6

Marta goes to the living room and looks through the hole in the door. It really was Hevandrique. She opens the door right away.

- Hello!- He greets her, giving her two kisses.

-Hi!

Hevandrique had also spruced up the look, putting on a white shirt, a gray blazer and blue jeans. He seemed to have shortened his black hair, enhancing his pale eyes even more.

- You can come in and sit down, she's coming soon.

- Thanks. Do you both live here?

- Yes, no… Sometimes we sleep together.- Marta says, surprising Hevandrique.- We don't sleep together the way you're thinking.- She corrects her, smiling.

- I know.

- Sometimes I stay to give you some support, given this new situation. And you, are you a doctor?- Marta asks, trying to change the subject.

- I'm a psychologist.

- Well, my first option was Psychology, but I ended up choosing Economics.

- My first option was Medicine, but I was prevented from following that area, so I was forced to settle for Psychology.- Says Hevandrique.

- Hello!- She greets Joana, leaving the room.

- Hello!- Hevandrique answers, getting up.

Exam

Hevandrique took Joana to Galatto. It wasn't his first choice, but they couldn't make a reservation at the restaurant they initially wanted. Hevandrique pulled out the chair for Joana to sit down.

- I like this place.- Joana says.

- Me too.

Joana began to feel a slight itching in her vagina. But she couldn't just, in the middle of dinner, put her hand there and scratch herself.

- What will it be?- Asks Hevandrique, with his eyes focused on Joana.

- You can suggest something.- Joana replies, who was losing the war against the allergy that wouldn't leave her alone, even getting her mouth trembling, and already with some sweat on her face, trying to contain herself so as not to make a scene.

- Are you okay?- Hevandrique asks, noticing Joana's distressed look.

- Yes!- She lies, taking a deep breath and faking a smile.

- If you want, you can go to the bathroom.- Hevandrique jokes, with an ironic smile.

Joana was thoughtful for a few seconds, but ended up getting up, informing that, in fact, she was already getting distressed.

Joana sat on the washstand and lifted her dress, then removed her panties and saw, with horror, her red vagina with small pimples around it. Worst of all, it was the unbearable odor she smelled. Unable to resist any longer, Joana makes the mistake of scratching herself, causing a bigger eruption of pimples and creating small wounds.

- My God!- Sighs.- Damn you, Marta!- Joana tried to get up, feeling immense pain as she tried to close her legs. The itching was increasing, now combined with the pain caused by the wounds. - Why didn't I bring my bag? - She complained to herself, sitting on the sink looking for a solution. After a lot of thinking,

Joana decides to get up despite the pain, trying to walk with her legs slightly spread. She stood looking at Hevandrique, who had his back to her, trying to think of a plausible explanation. Coincidentally,

Hevandrique turns around at that moment and finds Joana at the bathroom door. He gets up and goes to her.

- It's all right?

- I wanted to say yes, but I think I have to go home.- Joana answers, distressed, trying to control herself not to stick her hand under her dress and start scratching herself right there, in front of everyone.

- Of course, walk to the car and I'll get our things.- Hevandrique says, heading to the table.

Joana tried to take a step, but apparently it created a huge wound in her vagina, so much so that she couldn't even walk. She felt the allergy spreading to other parts where she'd swiped the blade, such as her butt and groin. Starting there she also felt an unbearable itching.

- What happened?- Hevandrique asks when he sees Joana still in the same place.

- I don't think I can walk.- Joana confesses, scratching her forehead, embarrassed.

- But why? What happened?

- I have an allergy, which makes it impossible for me to move.

Hevandrique puts Joana's suitcase around her neck and helps her put on her coat.

- Come, I'll take you on my lap.- Offer.

- I don't think that will be possible either, because that would mean closing my legs, something I can't do either.

- Ah, you just can't close your legs?- He says, confused.

- Yes.

- And if you go to my piggyback? - Joana shakes her head, saying that it wouldn't be possible either. - Then wait here, I'll be right back.- Hevandrique says, leaving quickly without looking back.

Joana waited for Hevandrique, distressed, with her private parts on fire.

3

- Where are you? - Joana whispers, when, twenty minutes later, Hevandrique arrives with a wheelchair, leaving Joana more relieved.

After sitting down, Hevandrique guides you to the car. There, he placed her in the car as carefully as possible, then put the wheelchair in the trunk, and they were off as quickly as possible.

- We had to go in the other direction.- Joana says.

- Let's go to the hospital.

- No! It's not necessary!- Joana replies, distressed.

- You're not well and you don't want to go to the hospital?

- It's just a small problem, I'll solve it later.

Hevandrique stops the car next to a building, which has a no parking sign.

-Let me see.- Hevandrique says, turning on the light.

- What?- Joana says, distressed, putting her hands on her legs. Hevandrique lowered Joana's chair, trying to lift her dress, but Joana stopped him. - What do you think you're doing?- She screams.

- You're not well, I'm a doctor and I can help.

- You're a psychologist!

- But I'm an expert in first aid.

- No, no! Get your hands off my dress!- Joana shouts again.

- Calm down, I'll just see.- Hevandrique manages to pull Joana's dress up, trying to bend down to see what was going on between her legs.

- Stop it, I'll never talk to you again!- Joana shouts, but without much effect.

When they hear a knock on the car window, Hevandrique lets go of Joana, who immediately lowers her dress, as well as the car window.

- Hello.- Says a policeman, leaning on the car window, leaning against Joana.

- I'll have to fine you for two reasons. For having sex in the car and parking in a no-go zone. And, by the way, can you give me your identification documents and driver's license. And get out of the car, please.

Hevandrique got out of the car immediately, walking around to speak to the agent.

- I think it's a mistake, we weren't having sex in the car!

- I bet she had the car seat down because she was very sleepy ...- Ironizes the agent.

- I know it seems strange, but she is feeling sick and I was trying to help her.- The policeman looked at Hevandrique, with a face that says, I don't believe you, and without further arguments, Hevandrique received the fine and returned to the car.

- Did he fine you?- Joana asks.

- Clear! If you weren't so stubborn, maybe we wouldn't be in this situation.

- The fault is mine? I said I didn't want to, you insisted!

Hevandrique took off before another policeman showed up to fine him.

- I'm not going out.- Joana says.

- But you need to go to the doctor.

- No!

- Look, we have HIV. We don't have 100% health. Our immunity is weaker and even a small problem, like a simple flu, we have to look for a doctor. So, please...-Joana looked at Hevandrique for a few minutes, wondering whether or not she should go through this embarrassment.

-It's fine.- She ended up giving in.

Joana was lying on the hospital bed to rest after the doctor applied an ointment that relieved the pain, leaving her more relaxed. The good thing is that Hevandrique didn't see her ugly vagina, as she only accepted to be examined if he stayed outside the room.

Hevandrique finally enters the room, pulling out a chair and sitting next to Joana.

- You're allergic to blades, but you still used them?- Asks Hevandrique, with a huge astonishment mirrored on his face. Joana tried to control herself, so as not to curse the doctor who attended to her.

- How did you know that?- Joana asks, gritting her teeth.

- The doctor who examined you studied with me in college and we happen to be kind of best friends.

Joana turned away, turning her back to Hevandrique, not knowing what to do, as the feeling of embarrassment was too great.

- Why did you do the waxing?- He asks, in a joking tone.

- Go away, I want to sleep!- Joana refutes, avoiding answering the question.

- Look, he's gone to sleep with me, it wasn't necessary. I'm difficult and I only sleep with women after a month.

Joana took the pillow and sent it against Hevandrique.

- Go away!- She yelled.

- Calm down!- He says, with an irritating smile.

- Now!- Joana asks again, screaming.

Timidly

Joana put on a wide black dress with white polka dots that reached her knees, black ballerinas and a white coat. On her face, just foundation and pink lipstick. Marta, on the other hand, wanted to rock as the hostess of the party, putting on blue jeans, a white blouse with a lot of neckline, black high shoes and a black blouse. She did a full makeup, including false eyebrows, and carrying the red lipstick to the extreme.

- Am I very simple?- She asks Joana.

- You're going to your boyfriend's birthday dinner, you're not going to your engagement!- Joana says, with a face of few friends.

- I know. But you know it's recent, and we don't see each other much because he's always in the hospital, and only his closest friends and family will be there. I cannot pass up this opportunity to conquer them all.

- Let's go, otherwise I'll give up going soon.- Joana says, still annoyed with Hevandrique for having humiliated her so much.

- I bet I know what the reason is. But why don't you call him?

- He should call, not me! He was the one who was an idiot, making me feel like a jerk. All that was left was to say that it was because I was so hasty that I caught this disease.

- No need to exaggerate, I bet he was just kidding and besides, he called. He called three times and all on the same day.

- I think we'd better get going, I'm getting bored already.

Joana and Marta arrived at Sabor Mineiro and, as soon as Marta saw António, she gave him a kiss and a gift she had bought him.

Joana looked at António for a long time, she knew she knew him, she had already seen that face somewhere. He looked like an average Portuguese man, 5'7" tall, with black hair and dark brown eyes, a medium to large beard. Where had she seen this man before?

- Come on Joana.- Marta says.

-Hello António, I'm Joana.- she introduces herself, greeting with two kisses.

~I know you.~ António says.~ Joana was surprised, as she thought she had only seen him on the street, once, having had his face in her head, but after all she was wrong.

~ Serious?

~ Two weeks ago you went to the hospital with Hevandrique and I attended to you.~ Joana's mouth dropped open. António is Hevandrique's best friend, just today that she didn't have any patience to put up with Hevandrique.

~ Speaking of which, there it is.~ Antonio says.

Joana turns around, her heart pounding and she almost loses consciousness when she sees Hevandrique and, especially, when she sees him with a girl.

3

Staring at him, stunned, she could only think of how much she wanted to disappear from there.

Hevandrique looks at her and smiles, making Joana even more angry.

~ Look who's here!~ He says, with his typical smile.

At that moment, Hevandrique's smile turned out to have a double effect, as Joana was both angry and, at the same time, melted by his charm. Dark, damp hair, like someone's hair just out of a shower, and eyes looking even greener at night. Perhaps because of the black clothes she was wearing, which made him even more attractive, much to Joana's misfortune.

~ Let's sit down.~ Antonio says.

~ Samira and Tereza?~ Hevandrique asks.

~ Neither of them confirmed it.~ Answers António.

Hevandrique sat next to Elisabeth, the woman who came with him, while António sat in the middle of Marta and Joana.

~ The world is quite small...~ Hevandrique comments, making Joana even more angry, because she was right in front of Hevandrique. But she almost couldn't look him in the eye. Keeping her face down and looking at her empty plate.

~ Do you know them?~ Elisabeth asks.

~ Yes.

~ I'm going to the bathroom.~ Joana says, getting up.

~ Of course, we'll wait for you. Try not to arrive until dessert time.~ Upon hearing Hevandrique speak, Joana shoots him a glare that leaves him silent, but immediately apologizing.

Joana takes two steps and comes back, grabbing her suitcase, and then leaves.

- Joana!- Marta shouts, getting up.

- Let me go.- Says Hevandrique, going after Joana.

- Wait!- asks Hevandrique, grabbing Joana's hand and preventing her from getting into the car.

- What is it? - Joana shouts, pulling her arm violently. - I thought you liked me, but then you treat me as if I were just another person, without even an apology. Today you show up here with another girl and, on top of that, do you want to make silly jokes?- Hevandrique looks at Joana, amazed, not knowing what to say.

- I called you...- He finishes saying, softly.

- You called three times and then you didn't hear from me for two weeks. I never thought I'd fall in love with an idiot like you.- Hevandrique smiles, making Joana angrier.- You're laughing, on top of that!?- Accuses Joana, annoyed.

-It's not every day you hear a woman say she's in love with you!

- You are so irritating...- Joana replies, between her teeth.

- I know.- Hevandrique pulls Joana to her side and tries to give her a kiss, but Joana turns her face away, trying to push him away, but without great success, as Hevandrique grabbed her face and managed to steal a kiss from her. kiss.

- Don't touch me!- Joana says, pushing him away.

- Do you know that we are putting on a show here on the street? Everyone is looking at us.- Joana looked around her and, indeed, there was a large group of people standing there looking at them. Angrily, Joana opens the car, which Hevandrique then closes again.

- She's just a friend. We also studied together in college, and I didn't call back because I wanted to give you a break.

- Let go of my car door.

- I can even leave, but only if you promise not to leave.

- I'm the one who decides that.

-I like you too.- She admits, removing her hand from Joana's car door. She stood there, not knowing what to do, and Hevandrique stayed behind her. Just looking at her.

- But?!- Suddenly shouts Samira, one of Hevandrique's friends. Samira, another one of his friends.

-Hello Samira.- He greets her, giving her two kisses.- Joana turned to see who she was and Hevandrique introduced her, telling her that

Joana was his new girlfriend. At that moment, he takes Joana's hand and goes back inside the restaurant.

~ So you guys are going out?~ Samira asks.

~ Yes!~ Hevandrique answers.

~ Very cute!~ Praises Samira.

~ Look, I have something to tell you. I think Luís is coming here. I ran into him at the hospital and unintentionally told him about this dinner. I believe he self-invited.

~ It doesn't matter.~ Answers Hevandrique, nervous.

~ Speaking of him...~ Alert Samira.

~ Hello cousin!~ Luis says, turning around and smiling.

~ Hello Luis.

~ You've got a really cute girl! Does she know you have AIDS?~ He says, turning around and taking another sip of his beer. Joana looks at Hevandrique with a panicked face. Hevandrique pulls out a chair so she can sit down, then does the same without responding to her cousin.

~ I don't remember inviting you.~ António says.

~ What evil! We studied together, we are friends, it was the least I could do.

~ How is your treatment? You have to be very careful, at this time the flu can take you to the coffin.~ António gets up, sighing, asking Luís to leave.

~ What did I do? Can't I worry about my cousin?

~ You'll never get over that?~ Asks António.

~ I'm over it, buddy, don't worry.~ Luis replies, with a fake smile on his face. Hevandrique just looked like a child trying to contain the crying. ~ I'm even worried about my cousin... ~ He insists, with an ironic smile. ~ How's the illness? Has he already turned into AIDS?~ He says, looking at Hevandrique, with a raised voice, making everyone in the restaurant look at them. António threw the glass of beer in Luís' face, going for him. The two fell to the ground, António on top, punching Luís. Hevandrique got up and pulled his friend with the help of three restaurant employees, while Luís lay on the floor with his mouth full of blood.

~ You can only be sick.~ Antonio says, grabbing his things and leaving with Marta. When they reach the door, António turns around and asks his friends if they wouldn't come.

~ Yes, of course!~ Samira replies.

~ Let's go, Hevandrique?~ Asks Elisabeth.

- You can walk, I'll pay for the damages.- Says Hevandrique, looking down at Luís, who was still lying on the floor, looking at the ceiling and with a smile on his lips, looking like a psychopath.

- Come on, get up.- Samira says, looking at Luís.

- It seems to me that I have been beaten, I need to rest.

- For God's sake, get out of there! You've already brought a lot of problems.- Says Elisabeth.

Luís gets up and stands looking at Elisabeth, with an unfriendly face, giving the feeling that he could attack her at any moment.

- Do you think I'm the culprit?- He says, already changing the tone of his voice once again.

- I'm sorry, gentlemen, but you'll have to leave.- Informs one of the employees.

- I didn't even have to say it.- Luís answers, leaving the restaurant.

6

As they leave the restaurant, the three find Luís leaning against Hevandrique's car, smoking a cigarette.

- Really?- Samira says in disbelief.

- What are you still doing here?- Elisabeth asks.

- Smoking. Also, I need to go home with my cousin.

- I'll take you to the house.- Samira says.

- No.- He refuses, taking another puff on his cigarette.

Joana watched Luis. He looked like a normal guy, blond, with light brown eyes, well dressed, in jeans, a white shirt and a gray suit coat. He wore black shoes and he didn't look crazy, he was even a very attractive man. Looking at him, standing there smoking, she didn't even look like the same person who had made all that scandal at the restaurant.

- Please...- Begs Samira.

- Damn it...- says Luís, throwing his cigarette to the floor. Then he looks at Joana... - Be very careful with my cousin. He's always surrounded by women, he's a kind of HIV-positive Don Juan. They all love him, even after they find out he's contaminated. I even imagine that it must be the illness that makes him even more attractive, it just can!- Joana sighs, starting to get nervous.- And do you know one more thing? He's already been with these two.- Lance, still, Luís, with an evil smile on his lips. Samira starts to leave, nervous and walking as fast as she can.

- Wait for me!- Luis shouts.

- I'm walking too Joana...- Elisabeth says shyly.- Sorry for all this confusion.

Hevandrique leaves the restaurant after fifteen minutes and opens the car, entering without saying a word. Joana looks at him from outside the car, with a face of few friends.

\- Shall we go?- Hevandrique asks, pressing his face to the window.

\- I think we need to talk.- He gets out of the car and leans his arms against the door, looking at Joana.

\- Do you really want to talk now, with this cold?

\- What was that that happened in there? Why does your cousin hate you so much? From what you've told me, you had every right to hate him, not the other way around. Then why? What did you do to him to make him feel all this anger towards you?

\- First, this is the past, and second, I'm not going to talk about my past with you.

\- What?- Joana says, surprised and shocked by Hevandrique's words.

-Let's go.- She finishes, getting into the car.

\- Having walked with all your friends is also in the past?

\- Are you going in or not?

\- No.

Hevandrique starts the car, leaving Joana there, completely flabbergasted. Not remotely, not even close, she believes that this is happening to her.

She waited an hour for Hevandrique, hoping he would return, but to her surprise, he didn't.

Apathy

- Did he leave you alone?- Asked Marta, who was almost choking on her glass of milk.

- How disgusting!- Joana reacts, seeing her friend spitting the milk she had in her mouth into the glass.- You'll have to buy me a new glass!- Joana warns, getting up from the table and lying down on the sofa.

-Hasn't he called yet?- Marta asks, approaching Joana as she sits next to her, at the bottom of the sofa.

-He didn't call or answer my call. When I tried to call him, nothing!

- And now?- Marta asks.

- And now it's over. He thinks he can play with me, as he did with the others, but he is sorely mistaken.

- Are you waiting for someone?- Marta asks, hearing the bell ring.

- No! Maybe it's some traveling salesman or an evangelist.

- Leave it alone, and I'll go see it.- Marta offers, who is surprised when she opens the door and finds Hevandrique.

- You?

- Hello, Martha.

- You can come in, she's in the room. I was already on my way out.

Hevandrique goes to the living room and finds Joana lying on the sofa, standing there looking at her.

- Who was it?- Joana asks, still with her eyes closed.

- It's me.- Answers Hevandrique.

Hearing his voice, Joana gets up, facing Hevandrique, trying to smooth her disheveled hair.

-What are you doing here?-She asks, forcing a serious face.

- You have cute pajamas.- Hevandrique says, with his playful smile, when he sees Joana's winter pajamas.

- I didn't ask your opinion about my pajamas.

- I wanted to apologize.- He says, now with a more serious tone.

- You are not excused, now go away, I need to sleep.

- I'll wait here.

- I didn't ask you to stay here waiting for me, I just want you to go away.- Joana asks, heading to the room, irritated. In the bathroom, she takes off her pajamas and lies in the bathtub, trying to relax to the music on her cell phone. There she stayed for a few minutes, but the discomfort did not let her relax properly, so she got up and grabbed the towel. She leaves the bathroom and is startled to see Hevandrique standing at the door.

- I thought I sent you away...

- You're right. I acted badly last night, I shouldn't have done that, it's just that I'm not ready to talk about that dark part of my past yet. It's something I know I did wrong, and to this day it still haunts me.

- You can stop talking. I already told you to go away, I don't want to know anymore.- Hevandrique took a step forward, making Joana, in despair, beg him not to come any closer.

-Why?-She asks, continuing to advance, slowly.

-Because the house is mine and I decide who can walk in it.- she replied, terrified. She knew the attraction that Hevandrique provoked in her, in such a way that she could barely contain herself. That scared her, in a strange way.- If you take one more step, I'll call the police.- Joana threatens, grabbing her cell phone.

Hevandrique pulled her by the arm and gave her a kiss, which Joana fully reciprocated, grabbing her tightly and squeezing her close to his body. With his right hand, he removed the towel, leaving her stark naked. Non stop kissing her. His hands caressing her private parts. Hevandrique realizes that Joana is already completely wet, making him excited, kissing her more and more, and laying her down on the bed, and making small sudden movements, leaving her more and more excited.- I'm ready...- Says Joana, with an almost pleading voice. Without thinking twice, Hevandrique opened his pants, and penetrated her, causing Joana to moan, in a sensual and exciting way, penetrating her with more and more force, without stopping kissing her. Hevandrique turned her over, placing her on all fours, first running his finger with plenty of saliva and then penetrating her. Joana had never done it this way, but she was so excited that she just had to endure the pain, which with time diminished, giving way to an even greater pleasure. Joana ended up lying down after reaching orgasm, while Hevandrique still continued to penetrate her, until she also reached ecstasy.

Joana opened her eyes and noticed that the room was dark. She took out her cell phone and was amazed that it was already 4:45 pm. She turns around and notices that Hevandrique is no longer beside her on the bed. He gets up. Covering herself with her robe, she goes into the living room, sighing in relief at the sight of Hevandrique lying on the sofa. He gets up when he hears Joana's footsteps approaching.

- Finally, you woke up!
- I thought you were already gone, what are you doing here yet?
- I can't believe you're still mad at me.
- Do you think!... That sex solves everything? You must be really bad used to it.- Hevandrique stood still, looking at Joana, without saying a single word.- Stop looking at me like that.- Joana says, trying to escape his gaze as she sits on the sofa, turning her face to the side. Hevandrique sighs and picks up his coat.

- Then I'm going home.- Joana refrained from asking him to stay. It was what she wanted, but she was still pretty hurt from the night before and she didn't want to just forget about it, as if nothing had happened. Pride kept her from asking him that.

Hevandrique goes to the door and opens it, informing him once again that he is leaving.

Joana gets up and asks him to wait.

- If you want I can order something for us to eat.- He says.

Hevandrique walks up to her and gives her a hug, leaving her there for a few minutes.

- Doesn't this door close anymore?- Joana pushes Hevandrique away. She couldn't believe it was Camila Filipa! Seeing her with her bags made her even more nervous.

- What are you doing here?- Joana says, surprised to see her sister.

- I told you that the father and the mother would travel, therefore, I will stay with you.

Joana had completely forgotten about that. At least today it didn't cross her mind that she will have to share the roof with her sister.

-But you had to warn!-She says, irritated.

- Hello... And who are you?- Filipa asks, looking at Hevandrique, with a face as if she is seeing an angel.

- He's a friend of mine, who was on his way out.- Hasten to answer, Joana.

- Yes sure. Nice to meet you. So, goodbye Joana.- Say goodbye to Hevandrique.

- I'll take you to the street.- Filipa says.

- Okay...- Answers Hevandrique, confused and looking sideways at Joana.

Filipa accompanied him, returning with a smile the size of the world.

- I'm glad he's your only friend.- She says happily, much to Joana's unhappiness.

3

Filipa puts on one of Joana's tracksuits and goes to her gym, after seeing a card from her sister's gym on top of the dresser.

She knew that Joana would be annoyed when she woke up, which really made her super excited.

When she arrives, she immediately sees Hevandrique, in the distance, running on the treadmill, and gets all excited, sitting on a bike, waiting for him to finish running.

Hevandrique takes a sip of his water and turns off the treadmill, wiping the sweat with the towel.

- Hello! - Says Hevandrique, surprised, but with a smile.

- Hello!...- Filipa replies, excited, getting up and going to meet Hevandrique, giving him a kiss on the cheek.

- Your sister?

- He's sleeping, I think he'll only come later.- Filipa says, trying to sketch an angelic face.

- Okay. I've already finished training, so I have to go home now.

- Already!?- Filipa asks, with a spoiled face.- I wanted to invite you to have breakfast with me...

- Next time, because I have to go to work.

- Okay, so see you tomorrow!- Hevandrique just waves and leaves.

Without training, Filipa returns home, looking great, and finds her sister waiting for her, sitting on the sofa.

- Hello Joana!- She says, with a smile.

- You go out, take my car, take my gym card. Where do you think your head is? Do you think this is all yours?- Asks Joana, increasingly upset.

-Sorry, today I'm very happy!-Says Filipa, sitting on the sofa and removing her sneakers.- You know, that friend of yours who was here yesterday?-She asks, looking Joana's eyes deep.

- What's wrong with him? - Joana says, already worried.

- He asked me out. We agreed to go get a cup of coffee. I still don't know what the best day will be. But I'll arrange with him and then we'll meet. Glad you don't go out!- Joana is totally upset and angry with Filipa, but mainly with Hevandrique. Without saying anything, she takes her keys and leaves, slamming the door in her rage, leaving Filipa happy as hell.

6

- I'll be right there!- Says Hevandrique, while trying to tie his tie, after Joana has rung the doorbell several times without stopping.

- Hi Joana, come in. Wait here just a minute.

- Wait!?- Hevandrique looks at her and notices her face with a few friends, as if something had really happened.

- What is it?- He asks, scared.

- It's okay that we only stayed once, and I don't even know if I consider you a friend or boyfriend, but how could you do this to me? Don't you have an ounce of consideration? - Joana says, already on the point of shedding a tear.

- What?- Hevandrique reacts, confused.

- Well, your cousin told me that you were a kind of Don Juan, and that it is very easy for you to play with women.

- Calm down!- Asks Hevandrique, without realizing anything.

- Why don't you come in? That way we can talk better ...- He says, trying to touch Joana, who immediately pushes him away.

- You know, you're the first person who interested me after my life changed completely. I thought that you, too, even a little bit, were interested in me, but it seems that I will always fall in love with the wrong people.

- Look Joana, I don't know what I did, so how about if you told me what happened?

- Do you know something? Ended! You stay in your corner and I'll stay in mine, but I ask you one thing, leave my sister away from this.- Joana turns around and calls the elevator.

- Wait a minute!- Hevandrique says, grabbing her arm, but Joana screams for him to let go.

- Okay, I'm sorry! I don't touch you anymore. But at least tell me what I did!- He begs, not understanding what Joana had said.

When the elevator arrived, Joana got in immediately. Hevandrique looked at his bare feet, but the elevator was about to close, so he decided to get in before he lost sight of Joana.

- Don't even think about following me!- Joana says.

- I first have to understand what happened.

On the third floor, a middle-aged couple enters, making Hevandrique even more nervous. Saying nothing, he massages his hair, trying to calm himself.

When the elevator opens, Joana tries to get out, following the couple, but Hevandrique grabs her by the arm, preventing her.

\- Let go of me!- She scolds, causing the couple to turn to him.

\- It's nothing.- Hevadrique says, kindly, to the couple, closing the elevator and loading, once again, on the seventh floor, to return to his apartment.

\- What do you think you're doing? I cry for help!

\- First tell me what I did, and only then I'll let you go.

\- You're not the boss of me! You know what you did, so leave me alone!- Joana says, trying to free herself, but without success, as Hevandrique had held her tightly.- You're squeezing me too much. You are hurting me!

\- All right, forgive me. But please tell me what's wrong with you being so upset with me!

\- Did you have to invite Filipa on a date, or whatever was going through your head?

\- Me what!?- Asks, gaping.- I didn't ask your sister out! I met her at the gym and she invited me to breakfast, which I declined, by the way. And besides, you introduced me to her as just your friend.- Joana breathes a sigh of relief upon hearing Hevandrique's words. Knowing her sister, it was quite possible that she was lying just to upset her.

\- Excuse me...- Joana says, looking at the floor.- Hevandrique also takes a deep breath, after Joana's apology.

\- Are you in a car?- He asks.

\- No. I forgot.

\- I'll drop you off at work. How about we arrange something for later tonight? I'm free from 10:30 am. Monday's session is faster.

\- Of course!- Joana accepts, with a smile.

Repentance

With a smile on his face, dressed in a full black suit, and shoes to match, Hevandrique was at Joana's door. With a sigh, he knocks, getting himself together.

- Go!- Hevandrique hears a voice that in no way resembles Joana's. It's Filipa, who opens the door and smiles. In a white, knee-length, half-transparent evening dress, crossing her right hand at her waist so that the robe no longer covered her breasts, which were almost on display.

- Hello.- Hevandrique says, faking a smile to camouflage his nervousness.

- Hello, come in!- Filipa says, with a look of innocence.

- Of course.- He answers, walking towards the room.

- Your sister?

- She is coming. You can sit down.- She says, sitting on the couch and crossing her legs, exposing her thighs.

- Of course.- Hevandrique sits on one end of the sofa, trying to stay as far away from Filipa as possible, but that doesn't stop her from leaning right next to him, getting as close to him as possible.

- Can you bring me a glass of water, please? - asks Hevandrique, trying to keep her away.

- Clear.

Upon returning, Filipa appears without the robe that covered her transparent dress, leaving only in her nightgown, with her breasts crossing the fabric and her black panties also on display. Hevandrique tries to look away from Filipa's body, but it was impossible to deny that she had a phenomenal body, which made anyone sweat, mainly because of the mixture of sexy and innocent woman. Her blue eyes and blonde hair made her look like an angel, largely due to her small, pink lips.

-Here you go.- She says, going back to sit beside him.

- What time is your sister coming back?

- I don't know.- She says, pressing her mouth to Hevandrique's ear, making him shiver.

- I think I have to go do something.- Says Hevandrique, standing up.

Filipa gets up next to him, standing right in front of him.

~Of course, but I need an answer!...~She says, approaching even more and grabbing his tie.

- Yes? - Answers Hevandrique, trying to hide his nervousness.

- Are you and Joana walking?

- What did she tell you?--He asks, sitting on the couch.

- No... Categorically, no...- Filipa says, kneeling down, facing Hevandrique.

- Then that's it.

- So...... Are you free to hang out with whoever you want?- Alicia Camila Filipa, putting her mouth to Hevandrique's mouth.

- No!!!- He says, getting up and dodging Camila Filipa.

- How...... no?- She says, dumbfounded, not understanding.

- I have a girlfriend and now I really need to go.- Hevandrique says, thinking it's the right thing to do before he can do any of the crazy things that already cross his mind.

Hevandrique heads for the door as quickly as possible, not looking back, taking a deep breath as he closes the door behind him.

3

Hevandrique was sitting in the cafe when Marta appeared. Waving to you from outside. He gets up and goes to the entrance, giving her two kisses and leads her to where he was sitting.

- Hi. So, is everything ok?- Marta asks, with a smile.

- Yes it is.

- So why did you ask me to come here?- Marta asks, placing her elbows on the table.- Hevandrique massages her eyes and then sighs, looking deep into Marta's eyes.

- I think Filipa is hitting on me.- Marta was unable to assimilate the information for some time. Filipa wasn't the type to hit on guys, it's not for nothing that, until today, she claimed to be a virgin.

- What?

- I know it's weird and I know you're not my friend, but you're Joana's friend and maybe you can tell me what to do. Yesterday I went to their house and she was there alone. From her conversation, from her attitude, I don't know. I think she was hitting on me." Marta turned around, leaning her back against the chair and sighing, not knowing what to say.

- It's like that, that's very strange, because I've never seen Filipa interested in a guy and she's always followed in her father's religious footsteps. I don't know if she ever wanted to have a relationship. There was already a little problem between her and Joana over a boy, but that was a long time ago and they were children, so I don't know what to tell you, I don't know if you should tell Joana, or, I don't know. ..- Says Marta, not wanting to tell Hevandrique the hatred that the sisters feel for each other.

- I understand, maybe it's just me… But tell me something, is it really true that she's a virgin?- Hevandrique asks, a little shocked.

- Yes, she is.- Marta says, smiling.

- How old is she?

- Twenty-five.-Hevandrique looked at Marta, looking like a geek.

- I never thought that there were virgin girls, over twenty years old. But now let's change the subject. Since we're both here at lunchtime, can we have lunch together? I'm hungry.- Invites Hevandrique.

- Of course.- Marta stopped to enjoy it, while Hevandrique chose his food, trying to analyze if he was really serious, since Filipa was never one to call boys, not even when they were little, except maybe Miguel, that made the sisters hate each other. However, Marta started to analyze his face, which is kind of round and thin, his hair is black and short. Even his mouth Marta looked at. She saw a very attractive young man. Anyone who saw him like that, she wouldn't imagine he had HIV. He would never cross any girl's mind. Hevandrique suddenly looks up at Marta. The blue eyes scared her in a strange way, without her being able to look away.

- Have you already chosen?- Hevandrique asks, smiling. That smile that Joana claimed left her over the moon. At that moment, in a strange way, that smile made Marta's heart race.

- Do you want me to suggest you?- He says, without ever closing the flirty smile.

- No, I think I'll keep the dish of the day. I'll just go to the bathroom in a moment, I'll be right back.- Marta says, moving away as fast as possible.

Marta looked at herself in the mirror and, for a few moments, saw Hevandrique's smile.

- Damn, what is happening to me?- She asks herself. She turns on the faucet and wets her face several times. When she found herself, she had practically removed all the makeup from her face.- It was just what I needed now...- She says, looking at the makeup left on the napkin.

Looking in her suitcase, she realizes she hadn't brought her makeup kit with her. Annoyed, she just tries to straighten her hair a little.

As she leaves the bathroom, she sees Hevandrique in the distance, completely absorbed in his cell phone, giving the impression that he is exchanging messages with someone.

\- I returned.

\- I already ordered the dish of the day, they will bring it soon.

\- Thanks.

\- You're cuter.

\- Serious? I had to wash her face, she was a little sleepy.

\- You always look cute.- He says, with the ravishing smile.

Whenever possible, Marta stopped to look at Hevandrique's mouth and, sometimes, at her eyes, since they were the two characteristics that most caught her attention, as well as her way of being and speaking. He was, in one way or another, charming.

\- I was talking to António a little while ago.

\- Serious?

\- Yeah, we're always talking.

\- How did you guys meet?

\- It's a funny story.- Says Hevandrique, resting his elbows on the table.- I think I have some luck. I'm very good with girls. You may not believe it, because you will never fall in love with me, but I am a guy who attracts women a lot.- Hevandrique continues, in a playful tone. And deep down, Marta agrees with everything he says.

\- And Antonio never went?

\- He was always shy, we met in junior year of high school. As everyone suspected that I had HIV, especially the boys, although no one could confirm it, I never had any friends. But, on the other hand, I had friends and one of them was a girl that António liked. One day he came to me and said that he liked her and that I should walk away, but to his surprise I said I could help. It was in a way of helping him that we became friends. The sad part is that he couldn't keep her, but in the meantime, we've gained this friendship. When he discovered my pills in my bag, I thought he would tell everyone, but he didn't, although he walked away a bit, but then he said he accepted me anyway and we've maintained our friendship ever since. We went to the same college and he even learned to fight because once a group of boys found out I had HIV and it started to plague my life. One day I was beaten up, I had to miss a year of school and everything, because an HIV patient has a very weak immunity, and anything makes him sick, from a simple cold to a serious illness. So he started training in martial arts and when I got better he always walked with me. One day, we saw the boys again, it was an exciting thing, while I just wanted to run away, António finished them off. That's when he became my hero, my guardian angel, we just needed to get married.- Hevandrique jokes.

- Wow!- Marta comments.

- He's my best friend. After my uncle, he is at the top of my life, I would do anything for him, because I know he would do the same. I always say that if he were gay, I would marry him, even though he's heterosexual.- Says Hevandrique, smiling.

- See if one day you don't get married!- Marta jokes.

- Who knows! But seriously, he's a spectacular person and so are you, I hope the two of you manage to work out.

- So you are the perfect friends, you must never have had a fight.

- Of course I have. The bad thing about best friends is that there's always a friend cuter than the other, and I've always been the cutest.- Hevandrique says, jokingly, making a sexy face.- Seriously now, he punched me once. , I thought my teeth had all come out of my mouth, but luckily it was only one, and it wasn't the front one.- Marta looks at Hevandrique, amazed, and smiles.

- You're too squeamish!

- Very! António is the strongest person in the world, he may not seem like it, because he is thin and short, but he is. I'm taller and I look stronger, but this is all an impression, it's just an optical illusion.

- Don't overdo it either!

- Seriously! I would never fight him. First because he is my brother, second because he is very strong, he did Kung Fu, Karate, Jiu-jitsu, and another art that I never remember the name of.

- Stop beating around the bush and tell me why he hit you.

- It was because it seems that the girl he was with liked me and, during a party, she gave me a kiss and he saw it. When I realized, he was already on the ground, with his mouth full of blood and with tears in his eyes... end!

Marta couldn't contain her smile and spent a few minutes laughing at Hevandrique.

- Don't laugh, your boyfriend is a monster.

- But all you had to do was tell her that you have HIV and the matter was resolved.

- I don't tell everyone I have HIV. It's not out of shame, but for privacy reasons. Of course, at the time, it was out of shame. I was twenty-one years old and it wasn't good for people to know I was sick, because they were afraid, or rather, they still are, but the funny thing is that I don't transmit the virus.- Marta looked confused at Hevandrique, without understanding what he had just said. - You've never heard of that either, have you? It's like this, if I have sex with women without a condom, I don't transmit the virus. I've done it once, but it's something I'd rather not risk, just in case, and also so she doesn't go into shock when she finds out she's slept with a boy who has HIV.

- That is true?

- And yes. A pity that in Joana's case it is not like that, but mine is. We are few, but we exist, if you want, we can experiment.- Says Hevandrique, looking at Marta with a seductive look. In turn, Marta turned as white as paper, not only because of Hevandrique's proposal, but because he put his face to hers...- I'm kidding! You don't need to have a stroke right here and now.- He says, smiling and taking a sip of his beer.

- I'm not going to have a stroke.- Marta replies, embarrassed.

- I like you.- Hevandrique says, making Marta even paler. Deep down, she was perfectly aware that it was just friendship, but even so, she was annoyed and couldn't answer.- We can be friends too, since you date my best friend and I date yours, although I don't I'm sure what we have can be called dating.

- Of course I do.- Marta replies, taking a sip of the juice.

- I enjoyed your company and would love to go out with you more often. We could even arrange group outings, it would be cool, although António doesn't like that very much.

- Sure, that would be great. But now I have to go.- Hevandrique wanted to offer a ride to Marta, but she was too confused to accept to stay one more minute next to Hevandrique. She had been with him a few times before, but why is it that now, that they are alone, does he attract her in any way?

6

Today was another day of meetings, but everyone was in a bad mood. When Joana entered, they were all bowed down, each one in a corner, all thoughtful. Mariana looked like she had been crying, Francisco also looked sad. In the background, the general mood was heavy. When Hevandrique arrived, everyone did the usual circle.

- Hello everyone, I know today was a bad day, even more so after what happened to Tomás.- Joana was confused, but at the same time scared.

-What happened to Tomás?-She ends up asking.

However, there is a knock on the door. Francisco gets up and goes to open it. It was Thiago, who sat down, not saying a single word. Everyone looks at him with pity.

-What is it?- He says, trying to hold back the tears.- Looking at everyone, Thiago starts to cry. It was the first time he had shown any emotion or sign of weakness and everyone felt sorry for him. Joana looked at him, nervous, afraid of what could have happened. - I'm going to give my testimony. When we turned eighteen, Tomás and I went to a disco and wanted to celebrate big. That's when, by my idea, we went to a brothel. Tomás accompanied me and there we found a very beautiful girl, who caught our attention. She looked like a goddess, with drop-dead gorgeous brown eyes that matched her beauty perfectly. The typical African braids made her even more beautiful. She sat next to us and we started talking. Her massive chest captured my attention and certainly his as well. She nor she looked like a whore. We were so excited that we didn't even think twice when she told us that she wanted to have a threesome with us. It was the first time we shared a girl, that we didn't even think about the possible consequences. We slept with her without using a condom. It was only some time later, when we decided to go back there, that we found out that she had been expelled for having HIV. Our world fell at that moment. We couldn't believe it. Tomás panicked, because he remembered that we hadn't used protection. This panic took hold in such a way that he began to cry and scream. The next day we both went for the test. It came back positive and the doctor advised us to come here. We promised each other that we would never tell anyone about our situation.- Thiago paused, trying to swallow some of the crying and wiping the tears that were already running down his face.

- If you're not well, you can stop for a moment.- Hevandrique says.

- No, I'm fine.- Thiago replies.- Thomas started going out with a girl, but he told me he didn't do anything with her, when I found out that, after all, he was hanging out with her and three others. I asked him what he was doing and he replied that if he had it, then everyone should have it. It felt like those were my words. I was the one who planned to contaminate the entire planet, not him, he always advised me. I tried to get him to stop, but I couldn't convince him. I ended up having to tell the girls he was with. Luckily, none of them had slept with him yet, but one ended up telling the whole school...- After that statement, Thiago pauses and starts crying again.- Everyone made fun of him and his parents wanted him to be expelled, for having tried to expose several teenagers to the disease. Nobody approached him and he didn't want to talk to me. The strangest thing is that he didn't reveal to anyone that I was infected too. That's something I'll always ask myself, why would he never tell me that. That's what scares me the most. In the farewell note he apologized to me. I owed him a big apology, not the other way around. I can't sleep, I can't stop crying. He was more than my friend, he was a brother and I don't know how I'm going to live without him. I don't know what to do.- Joana started to cry. She was the only one who still didn't know what had happened.

- He's going to wake up.- Try to comfort Hevandrique.

-What?- Asks Joana.

-He threw himself from the building, but he's not dead, he went into a coma.- Hevandrique explains.

- He's been like this for a week, sooner or later, they'll definitely turn off the machines, I know they will, and my friend will be gone forever. I won't know what to do. If I, at least, hadn't told the girls he had the disease, he...

- He could contaminate three girls, you acted in the most responsible way possible.- Hevandrique interrupts.

- What's the use?- Says Thiago, getting up from his chair and changing his tone of voice, seeming that, at any moment, he would go after Hevandrique.- I will always regret having told those idiots that my friend had HIV. I had to let them be contaminated, because now they've left me with this weight on my conscience, because, one way or another, I killed my friend, I'm the one to blame. But, also, what gave me to play the good Samaritan and help those bastards?-He continues, his voice lowered and already choked with sobs, from crying so much.

- At this moment, you may not even realize the great good you have done, but later on, you will recognize that you made the right choice. -No, I didn't!-She says, crying and kneeling down. Hevandrique went to him and gave him a hug. Thiago really seemed to need that hug. - I don't want him to die! Forgive me God, for all the times I cursed you.- She says, crying, while hugging Hevandrique.

The game

- Come on!- Hevandrique shouts, wrapping himself in a towel, leaving his wet chest exposed. When opening the door, he comes across Filipa. Confused and with a strange fear, he smiles to hide it.

- Can I come in?- Filipa asks, with an angel's voice. Hevandrique scratches her neck, trying to think of what to do to get her out of the way.

- I don't think it's a good idea.- She says, trying not to look at her bare legs, due to the short, tight dress, clinging to her body, under a completely unbuttoned overcoat.

-It's fast, what I have to tell you.- he affirms, walking towards the room, without waiting for authorization. Hevandrique followed with shorter steps, scratching her head with nervousness. Filipa sat on the sofa, removing her coat and crossing her legs. The fact that he knew she was a virgin, in a strange way, attracted him, but he tried to think about Joana, since they were sisters and she would certainly never forgive him. And, deep down, Hevandrique knew he would never sleep with her, mainly because of Joana, and also because he didn't like going out with two sisters at the same time.

- I'll be right back. - Says Hevandrique, heading to the room and wearing a dressing gown, taking the opportunity to send a message to Marta. She was the only person that came to his mind and the only one who could help him, as he didn't want to cause a misunderstanding between Joana and Filipa.

- Here I am.- He says, sitting in an armchair that was right in front of the sofa, where Filipa was sitting.

- I want to invite you.

-An invitation?-Hevandrique repeats, with a frightened look, unable to hide the fear he felt with the question.

- Will you come with me to church?- Hevandrique was speechless.

- Tomorrow there will be a service for couples, or future couples, and I would very much like you to go with me. -Prays Filipa, kneeling before Hevandrique and placing her hands on his legs.

- And what are we going to do at the couples service?- He asks, with a serious face.

- I want us to become a couple.- Hevandrique gets up and goes behind the armchair, trying to keep his distance from Filipa. As much as he has no intention of sleeping with Filipa, she was very pretty and he knew accidents happen.

- You know, I'm already with someone, so...- Filipa approached Hevandrique and took his hand, which was resting on the armchair, staying, once again, very close to him.

- It doesn't matter.- She says, with an angel's face, preventing Hevandrique from finishing the sentence. o without reaction, not even when she moved her lips to his. When Filipa prepared to intensify the kiss, placing her tongue in Hevandrique's mouth, he grabbed her face, preventing her from bringing their mouths closer, and sighs.

- I think you better go.

- But why?

- You're too innocent for me to do bad things to you.

- Who guarantees you? I know you want me, or at least you want me, so let yourself go.- Provokes Filipa, trying to give her one more kiss, when the doorbell rings.

- I have to answer.- He says, heading for the door, thanking God.

-Hello Marta.- Greets nervously.- Filipa goes to the door to see who she was, and is surprised to see Marta.

- What are you doing here?- Marta asks.

- I have to ask what are you doing here? Do you happen to walk?

- No.- Marta replies.- He's with your sister.

- That's a lie.

- No, it's not.- Hevandrique intervenes.- Filipa looks at him, with the face of a child who has lost the candy, almost knocking Marta down as she leaves without looking back.

- Thank you very much!- Hevandrique says, sighing.

- What happened here?- Marta asks, looking at Hevandrique's small erection, which can be seen through the robe.

- Anything. I'll be right there.- She says, covering herself with her hands.

Not long after, Hevandrique comes out again, already wearing shorts, a shirt and flip-flops, coat in hand and at a hurried pace.

- What is it?- Marta asks, confused.

- Joana is in the hospital.- Answers Hevandrique, nervous, heading for the door. Marta follows him and they both head to the hospital as quickly as possible.

3

When he sees António, Hevandrique goes to him immediately.

- How is she?

- Why are you two together?- Asks António, with a face of few friends.

- It's a long story, I'll tell you everything later.- Hevandrique says nervously.

- She's fine, you can come in.

- Thank you.- Marta also wanted to go in, but António asked to speak with her, grabbing her arm and preventing her from passing.

Joana was on an IV, with swollen eyes. Hevandrique approached, placing his hand on top of Joana's.

- What's it?

- I just had the flu, I never thought that a flu would make me so bad.- Joana says, with her eyes full of tears.- I know I've been told that my immune system is weak, but I never thought that something so small, that I previously overcame with some pills, now be reason for me to go to the hospital. I never felt like this in my life, I thought I was going to die.

- I know.- Hevandrique says, giving him a hug.

- How did you manage to live so long with this disease?- Joana asks, responding to the hug.

- It's really a horrible thing, but it's not the end of the world. You'll get over it, don't worry. You just need extra care. We are healthy people, but we have to be more careful.- She says, stroking his hair.

Joana and Hevandrique went to Tomás' room and there Thiago was, sitting looking at his friend, concentrated, in the hope that he would open his eyes. Thiago hardly left his friend's side since the day of the tragedy.

- Hi Thiago. Say hello to Joana.

- Hello.- He replies, without taking his eyes off his friend.

- Don't worry, he'll get better.- Joana says, trying to comfort the young man.

- Only three weeks to go. In a little while, he will die.- She says, with a hoarse voice, of someone who spent the whole night crying.

- Let's pray. I know he will wake up.

- I pray every day, I go to church every day, I make promises, I'm fasting, but nothing happens. We've known each other since elementary school. Since then, we have never been apart. We are so different from each other that everyone asks how we are friends. He was always calm and I was aggressive, he was always forgiving while I sought revenge, he always studied and I didn't, he demanded that they change his name from Tomás to Thomas, just to match mine. He was a geek, but he's one of the people I like and admire the most, I don't think it's fair that something like that can happen to him. I saw myself in that state, but I never thought he was the one in a hospital bed. I always imagined that I would do what he did. How funny things are...

- Everything will work out. I'm going to pray too.- Joana says.

- Me too.- Support Hevandrique.

6

Cassandra opens the door, and arrives with a basket of fruit.

- Hi.

- Hello, how are you?

- Will you always be here?- Asks Thiago to Cassandra.

- You're ungrateful.

- I never asked you to come.

- But even so, I will continue to come. By the way, I brought some grapes, it's your favorite fruit.

- I don't want.

- You can land here, in this corner.- Joana intervenes.

-We'll walk.- Says Hevandrique.- Joana is receiving a saline solution and she can't stay here for long, but I pass by every now and then.

- Of course.- Says Thiago.

As they left, Joana felt a little dizzy, but Hevandrique carried her to the bedroom, placing her on the bed, as carefully as possible.

- I didn't know that Cassandra liked Thiago.

- Neither did I, I thought it was the other one, but then it started to be noticed that it was Thiago's. They even make a cute couple.- Answers Hevandrique.

- Yes, you are right.

- I'll talk to António and I'll be right back.- Hevandrique says, giving Joana a kiss. But without giving Hevandrique time to leave, António enters along with Marta, he placing himself on the right side of Joana's bed and she next to Hevandrique.

- I was going to meet you.

- I know.- Antonio says coldly.- You can go home now. I have already signed your release and you are released.- Antonio informs, turning around and heading back to the door.

- What is it, bro?- Hevandique says, trying to go after him.
- I have to work, you don't have to come after me.
- Did something happen?- Hevandrique asks Marta.
- We had a little disagreement.
- But is it something serious?
- Do you want Marta to tell you about her love life now?- Joana says.
- You're right, sorry, I'll be right back.
- He said he needs to work.- Joana says, grabbing his hand and preventing him from leaving.
- Of course.- He answers, but worried.

Hevandrique arrives at the house and finds the lights on. He goes to the kitchen and notices that the lights are on there too. He picks up the broom and grabs it with both hands, walking slowly into the room, which is untidy, with packets of cookies on the floor and cans of beer on the table. The television is on, an adult channel. He hears a shower noise and goes to the bedroom, seeing some pants and a white t-shirt on his bed, which can only be Luís's. Hevandrique goes to the living room and starts tidying it up, since Luis left it like that forever.

- Hello cousin.- says Luís, getting out of the shower, with a towel tied to his waist and another drying his hair.
- Hello Luís, what brings you here?- Luís turns around and sits on the sofa, changing the channel, since today there was an important game.
- If you go to the kitchen, bring me a beer.- Luis says, with the greatest of relaxation. Hevandrique brings two, sitting next to him, handing him a beer, opening the other.- You know you can't drink much.- Ironizes Luís.
- I know.- Hevandrique answers, with a dry smile.- Don't you tell me why you're here?
- Your uncle threw me out of the house, saying the usual shit. That I have to work, and blah blah. I think if I go back to the hospital, I end up killing someone.
- You can always be a paramedic, the last time you tried, you failed good.
- Don't try to have a friendly conversation with me, because you know it irritates me.
- As you wish.
- I stay in your room, I like your space.
-All right.- Hevandrique accedes, in the purest of calms.

Luís

~Are you okay?~Filipa asks her sister, who has a terrible face, since she still hasn't gotten better from the flu.

~ More or less.~ Joana replies, lying on the sofa with her eyes closed.

~ You do not work today?

~ Work, I just need to get some rest, but why?

~ Look, today I'm going out, at night you don't have to wait for me.

~ Where are you going?

~ It's none of your business.~ Filipa says, getting up towards Joana's room and opening her sister's suitcase, searching it until she finds 50 euros in one of her pockets. Then she opens her wallet and takes out another 100 euros in banknotes and 6 euros in coins. ~ I'm going out.

Filipa went to the Miss store, in Colombo, ready to conquer Hevandrique, whatever the cost. She didn't care if he was seeing her sister. Buying red lingerie, which the saleswoman recommended. Then she plucked her eyebrows, bought a red lipstick too, to match her lingerie. When she left the shopping center, she went to her second-to-last destination, the hairdressing salon, with the aim of having her hair dyed and cut, to look identical to her sister's, leaving her with a more adult face.

Filipa waited until 1 am and went to Hevandrique's house. Luckily, she found the bottom door open and only needed to go upstairs. Like the other times, she'd tucked only her lingerie under her overcoat. She knocked on the door and nothing. She kept knocking for five minutes until, finally, the door was opened. Throwing himself on top of Hevandrique. In the midst of the darkness, he just responded, thinking it was Joana, since now they both had the same hairstyle. Taking her to the bedroom, without stopping kissing her, he threw her on the bed. Climbing on top of her. Pulling hard on her panties. Leaving her almost naked. She was only wearing a bra.

~ Calm down, you're going to hurt me! ~ Filipa says, scared. ~ Without paying any attention to what she was saying, Hevandrique got up and took out a condom she had in her suitcase. He took off his pants, climbed back onto the bed and put his penis in Filipa's mouth, with the intention of forcing her to suck it. .

But he pushed her, put the condom on, but then Filipa realized that maybe it was a bad idea to continue, since he seemed too aggressive. - Hevandrique, no! Please.- Without paying any attention to what Filipa was saying, he placed himself on top of her and began to penetrate her. Penetrating her with such force, that Filipa only felt pain, so much pain, that she asked him to stop, but he didn't. But without success. He continued, until Luis woke up to the screams, slamming the bedroom door.

- Luís?- Between crying and pain, Filipa hears that voice coming from the other side of the door and screams for help. In a second the door is open, the lamp is lit, and he stops. After all, Filipa didn't realize that she was with the wrong man, Luís. Louis, not Hevandrique. There Filipa takes the opportunity to push him, covering herself and crying in fear. Crying. Crying incessantly. Crying. Crying inconsolably.

Filipa

Hevandrique sees Luís putting on his pants with a smile on his face. The bed was full of blood and Filipa was terrified, especially after realizing that she slept with the wrong person.

- What did you do?
- I didn't rape her, she jumped on me. Your girlfriend is a bitch!
-She is not Joana, she is her sister!-Screams Hevandrique.
Luís looks at Filipa, scared crying, and is speechless.
- Are you sleeping with both of them?
- Of course not! I don't know if you noticed, but she was a virgin, and you took her virginity in the worst way possible. Your problem is with me, you don't need to be involving other people.- Filipa got up, covering herself with the sheet, scared. Hevandrique wanted to take a step, but she yelled at him not to come any closer. - Calm down.
- If any of you approach me, I'll scream so much, that all the neighbors will wake up.- She says crying and shaking.
- Okay, fine, I'll call Joana to come get you.
- I want you two to get out of here now! Now!- He shouts, even louder.
- All right!- Hevandrique says, grabbing Luis' arm and leaving the room.
Hevandrique took a deep breath, sighing, not knowing what to do. Luís was also worried, especially after learning that she was a virgin. He always wanted revenge on his cousin, but he never thought of harming anyone who wasn't connected to him.
- Call António, and I'll call Joana.- Luís barely managed to call António, just thinking that, at any moment, he would be arrested. Maybe accused of rape. Start to panic. Seeing that his cousin was barely moving, Hevandrique called António first, asking him to come to his house urgently, and then he called Joana, asking only her to come as urgently as possible.
- Do you think I'm going to jail? I didn't know it was someone else, I swear.
- I know, but it all depends on how she's going to face the situation.

- Of course I'm going to jail.

- Calm down, now the damage has been done, go take a shower, to see if you get that blood out of your body.

Luis could barely move, Hevandrique had to accompany him to the bathroom and put him in the shower so he could take a shower.

3

Joana arrived first, as she lived near Hevandrique, and came with Marta, who was keeping her company.

- What's it?

- It's just that...- Hevandrique started, stuttering, not knowing where to start.- Filipa...

- What's wrong with Filipa?- Asks Joana, already worried.- Is she in the hospital? Answer me Hevandrique, you're making me nervous! Where is my sister?

- She's in my room.

- What?- Joana went to Hevandrique's room and the first thing that caught her attention was the bloody sheets. Already scared, she approaches and sees Filipa terrified in a corner, all shrunken and covered in blood. Joana approached and, seeing her sister, Filipa gives her a hug, trembling. - What is it?

- ...he, he, he...- Filipa stammered, unable to say a word. Joana let go of Filipa and went to the living room, finding Hevandrique talking to Marta. She leapt at him, punching and slapping him.

- What did you do?- Joana shouts.

- Calm down!- Marta says, trying to grab her friend.

- If you infected my sister, I'll kill you!- At this moment António enters and, without understanding anything, looks at Hevandrique, standing still, while Joana tried to attack him, and looks at Marta holding her friend, who seemed uncontrollable.

- Calm down.- António says, grabbing Joana.- What happened here?

- That crazy friend of yours raped my sister!- Then António let go of Joana but put himself in front of her, so she wouldn't pass.

- That's impossible.- Antonio says.

- Then go see my sister! She's on the floor, bleeding! Maybe, in his room!- António looked at Hevandrique, who also looked at him, without speaking a single word. Antonio knew there had to be an explanation, he knew Hevandrique and he would never do such a thing.

Hearing the shower running, the bag of clothes on the table, and Luís' cell phone, António already suspected what really happened. He went into the room with Joana and helped Filipa up.

- Where are you going?- Asks Hevandrique.

- To the hospital.- Antonio says.

- Can't this stop here?- Asks Hevandrique.

- What the fuck are you talking about?- Asks António.- You just need to take the blame yourself.- Hevandrique watched António take Filipa out, not knowing what to do, since Luís could even go to jail.

- I'll go with them.- Marta says to Hevandrique.

- Me too.- Says Hevandrique.

- No, you stay here!- Joana says, looking at him from the side, with that look so full of hate.

- Wait for me!- Hevandrique insists.

- Fuck! You're staying here!- Antonio says, leaving Hevandrique without reaction, standing still as they left the apartment.

Joana sat in the hospital canteen, crying, not knowing what to do or what to think. She didn't understand why Hevandrique attacked Filipa and, above all, she didn't understand why her sister went to Hevandrique's house.

- You are okay?- Antonio asks, giving him a glass of water.

- No. Thanks. How is she?

-She is already medicated and sleeping. Tomorrow the results of the rape test will be released.

- I don't know what to do, I can't understand! I don't know if I'm crying for him or for her, just thinking that he did that to her, I can only hate him, but on the other hand, for a few minutes I wish I could forget about it, until I asked Filipa to keep it a secret , said that she was not violated, just to think that, automatically, our relationship is over. It's something that makes me cry, am I being selfish to think like that?- Joana says, with her hands covering her face.

- One thing I can assure you. It wasn't him.- Joana looked at António in amazement.

- I know he's your friend, but it's all clear.

- Even if Filipa accuses him, I know he would never do that. And, mainly, because Luís was with him at home.

- For God's sake, at no time did I see anyone else at home.

- I'm sure, it can only be him. I noticed that Hevandrique's house was dirty, and Hevandrique would never leave his house dirty, that's Luis' thing.

- That doesn't justify.

- I saw a bag of clothes, which could only be Luís. Hevandrique is from Porto and would never need to see a game between Benfica and Sporting. And someone was taking a shower. Hevandrique uses Samsung, the only person I know who still uses Nokia is Luís. And that person can only be Luís, even if no one was home, I would prefer to believe that Filipa got crippled, or some other story, unless Hevandrique raped her. I know the friend I have and one thing I can guarantee you. He would never do such a thing.

The happiest man in the world

As soon as dawn broke, Hevandrique and Luis hit the road and headed for the hospital. When they arrived, they went to Antonio's office, which, luckily, was already there.

- How is she?- Asks Hevandrique.

- One thing I don't understand, why did you do that to Joana's sister? If it were Joana, I would understand, but now her sister, what would your logic be?- António asks, looking at Luís, confused.

- It was an accident.- Hevandrique says.

- What? Accident!?- Asks António with an ironic smile.- Are you going to side with him? Do you know that Joana is your girlfriend, or is the guilt you feel greater than what you feel for her?- Hevandrique was silent, not knowing how to respond.- You can be quite irritating. She's in room 17.- Informs António, sitting and turning around in his chair, with his back to both of them.

- I'll come talk to you later.- Hevandrique says.

When they arrive in the room, Hevandrique says that he would go in first, so that Filipa wouldn't panic when she saw Luís in front of her. He saw Joana sitting with her head on the bed, sleeping, and Marta was also sleeping on a sofa. Filipa was also still sleeping, everything indicated that Filipa had been sedated, and she wouldn't wake up anytime soon, since her face looked like the one she cried long before sleeping.

3

When Hevandrique closed the door, Joana woke up. Seeing Hevandrique, she got up without speaking, took his arm and led him out of the room. When leaving the room, she notices that Luís had also come.

- What is he doing here?

- I know he wasn't supposed to be here, but he came to apologize.

- What? It's not his fault!- Joana slaps Hevandrique's face and enters the room, slamming the door in his face.

Marta is startled and wakes up, seeing Joana nervous.

- What's it?

- He's here, do you believe it? And he brought his cousin! She even says that it's not his fault, that it was an accident.

- Maybe it's my fault.- Marta says.

-What?!-Joana asks, not understanding why her friend would say that.

- A while ago, Hevandrique spoke to me, saying that Filipa was hitting on him, but I didn't take him seriously. I thought maybe it was his paranoia. How could I have imagined that Filipa, who hated every man on the planet, would be interested in anyone?

- Why didn't you tell me anything?

- Because it wasn't important. You are living together and I thought it would make your sisterly relationship even worse.

- How?- Joana says, even more confused, shedding a tear.

- She went to Hevandrique's house and the only way he could get her out of there was to call me. Then I had proof that it was really true, because the way she was dressed, she didn't look like the Filipa we knew. She was wearing a tight, short dress. She even thought that I was the one who was with Hevandrique, but that it was you after all... I had to tell her that it was you and she left nervous.

- You should have told me all this, you are my friend!

- I know, sorry.

- Damn, what kind of person are you?- Joana left the room, nervous, and saw that Hevandrique and Luís were still there.

- Tell me what happened!- Joana demands, looking directly at Luís.

- I can try to explain.- Hevandrique intervenes.

- I'm not talking to you, I'm talking to your cousin.

- She appeared at night, all of a sudden. I opened the door and she jumped on top of me, and I thought it was you, so I slept with her, I didn't know she was a virgin, it never crossed my mind.

- And why did you think it was me? Why did you want to sleep with me?- Luís looked at Hevandrique, who was startled by Joana's question.

- Joana...- He tried to interrupt Hevandrique.

- I already said I'm talking to him, not you!

- This is something he has to talk about, not me.

- Then speak! - Joana says turning now to Hevandrique.

-That's beside the point.- He says.

- How? Does your cousin sleep or rape my sister, and you don't want to tell me everything? You can only be making fun of me!

97

- Your sister went looking for this.- Joana went on top of Hevandrique once again, slapping him, without him protecting himself or even showing signs of wanting to protect himself.

- Calm down.- Luis says, grabbing Joana.

- Don't touch me!- Joana shouts.

- You're both crazy, I bet your quirk must be that, each one sleeping with the other's girlfriend.- Joana enters the room, nervous, and asks Marta to leave.

- Joana...

- Get out!- She says, sitting up and looking at Filipa, who was sleeping like a rock. Without speaking a single word, Marta leaves the room, finding Hevandrique and Luís.

- Are you okay?- Marta asks, touching Hevandrique's face, which was red, because of Joana's cracking. Behind Marta was Antonio, who sees her touching Hevandrique's face, worried.

- António.- Hevandrique says. Nervously, Marta removes her hand from Hevandrique's face.

- It's him, I was right!!!- Antonio says. Marta didn't answer, just lowering her face.

- What did I do?- Asks Hevandrique, looking at Antonio.

- You keep quiet. Martha, answer me!

- Answer what?- Says Hevandrique.

- Damn, I told you not to meddle!- Antonio shouts. Seeing that it was serious, Hevandrique fell silent before Antonio screamed again and woke up all the patients.

A nurse passed, looking scared at Antonio, and immediately entered the room of one of the patients.

- I think you better not get involved in it.- Luis says in Hevandrique's ear.

- This is not something for us to talk about here.- Marta says. António shakes his head and turns around. Hevandrique goes after him, grabbing him by the shoulders, then Antonio turns and punches Hevandrique, who immediately falls, climbing on top of him, and delivering another. Louis tried to get him off Hevandrique, but without much success. Marta runs off to call security, while Luís tries to get him off Hevandrique, who couldn't defend himself from António's punches. With the noise, Joana leaves the room and tries to help Luís get António off Hevandrique, but without much success.

- You're going to kill him, you know how he was the last time you did that to him.- says Luís. Antonio stopped and looked at Hevandrique's bloodied face. Getting off him, he stood, for a moment, looking at Hevandrique, who was on the floor, unable to get up, clenching his teeth, trying not to cry. António turns around and goes to his room.

- Are you okay?- Joana asks, trying to wipe the blood with her blouse.

- I am.- He answers, without strength.

Marta arrived, already seeing Hevandrique sitting on the floor, along with Joana and Luis.

- What happened?- Asks a security guard.- Who did this to you?

- I just came from the street.- Says Hevandrique, trying to get up, but without much success.- I just need to wash my face.

- No, I'll call one of the nurses.- Marta says.

- But what happened?- Asks the security guard again.

- Nothing, she thought we were fighting, but it was a mistake, it was to call a nurse.- Luís says.- Come, I'll help you up.- Hevandrique leans on Luís, who helps him to go to the infirmary. .

- I'll go with you.- Joana says.

- No! Stay with your sister, she can wake up at any time.- Luis counters.

After they bandaged Hevandrique, the nurse said she didn't need stitches. Her face would be swollen for a few days, but then it would go away, with lots of ice and taking her prescribed pills.

- Thank you.- Says Hevandrique.

- What did you do to him? Are you going with her friend too? If I were António, I wouldn't be your friend anymore, it's the second girl who breaks up with him because of you.- Luis says, sitting on the bed next to Hevandrique's.

- I need to talk to him.- Says Hevandrique, trying to get up.

- You are an amazing person. I always thought you guys had something, Antonio is always fighting with everyone who treats you badly, and you're always after him, as if you depended on him for a living. When we were younger, I was sometimes jealous of you, but then I got used to it. But that's strange, that is, at this moment you forgot that you're bad with your girl, because António decided to be bad with you.

- Help me go talk to him.

- Rest, he'll come talk to you later. Let his anger at least end, because if he goes for you again, this time he'll kill you.- At this moment

Hevandrique lies down on the bed and asks Luís to leave him alone, turning around. to the opposite side.- Of course.- Says the cousin, getting up.- You know, after having slept with Filipa thinking it was Joana, I didn't feel well. I always wanted revenge on you, but when I thought I had achieved it, I saw that it was of no benefit to me. I think seven years is a long time to hold a grudge against a cousin. Right now, I wanted to forgive you and also apologize, because both today's incident, and maybe hers, was my fault. Blaming you was the only way I could get rid of my guilt. What hurt me the most was knowing that she preferred you over me. I remember I went to talk to her after all, and I said I forgave her, but she said she didn't want my forgiveness. That was what destroyed me, so I did what I did, I had to apologize to you, but pride and the desire to avenge me spoke louder than anything else.- As Luís spoke, Hevandrique held back. if not to cry, but when he noticed that his cousin was gone, he let out a cry.

- Hevandrique?- Hearing Joana's voice calling, Hevandrique stood up, wiping her tears and faking a smile.

- What's it?

- Are you okay?

- In some pain, but I am.

- Did something happen? You have tears in your eyes.- Joana says, sitting next to him.

- I just had a beating, of course I have to have tears in my eyes.- Hearing this, Joana couldn't contain herself and even had to smile.- You're laughing at someone who got beaten up by the man of iron!- Joana gave Hevandrique a hug, trying to comfort him.

- Right now, I should be upset with you, but I just want to comfort you.

- I'm very sorry.- Hevandrique says, returning the hug.

- I know.- Joana says, stroking his back.

6

Hevandrique and Joana lay down on the bed, looking at each other for a few minutes, not saying anything.

- When Luís told the whole school that I had HIV, I had the worst moments of my life. On the one hand, I understand Tomás for trying to end his life, because it's something horrible, nobody deserves to go through that. Because of this, my application for medical school was denied. I decided to take revenge on him, I was so angry, that I would be capable of anything, everything, to take revenge on him.- Hevandrique stopped, trying to contain the crying.

- If you don't want to tell me now, you can do it another time.

- No, I just need to control myself. Luís had a girlfriend, he was very happy, he had the woman in his life and he was studying medicine, he was healthy... He was the happiest man in the world, it was the first time he apologized for doing that to me, I saw that he was really sorry, but I was not willing to forgive him. I pretended I forgave him, and for a while we lived in peace, he was happy. But as for me, I didn't have any of that, so I decided to take away the thing that made him the most happy, the girl he loved. I seduced her, I don't know how she fell in love with me, and we had an affair without Luís knowing. I convinced her not to leave him, only she stayed with them both. The first time I slept with her, I filmed it and gave it to Luís as a gift. When he saw the tape, he was so angry, he went to her. They argued and he spread it to the whole school. Everyone saw that she slept with me and, when she realized that, she committed suicide. I don't know who is the main culprit, if it was me, if it was her, if it was Luís... What torments me is that I practically destroyed the lives of two people. They were happy and maybe she was still alive today. But, because of my envy, I practically ended her life, and Luís's too, because he later dropped out of school, started drinking, using drugs, had to be hospitalized several times in rehabilitation clinics and became in this Luís that everyone knows. I didn't want him to go through this when I did what I did. I felt like the worst person in the world. I was never able to ask for forgiveness as he deserves, because, as much as I put it in my head that it wasn't my fault, it was more my fault than Luís's, who shared it with everyone on the video.- Then Joana gave Hevandrique a hug, stroking his hair, trying to comfort him as he cried.

Sister's words

Joana was sitting watching TV when there was a knock on the door. When going to see who it was, Joana comes across Martino. After disappearing for several weeks, he returned, thinner and with some signs of punches to his face.

- What is it? - Joana asks worried, helping him to sit down.
- I'm fine, I just had an argument at the disco.
- But why did you come here? I said it was over between us.
- I know, but I don't want to live without you, give me one more chance, I swear I'll change.- Martino implores, kneeling before Joana.
- This time, it won't work. I no longer feel what I felt for you, now there's only a small physical attraction left, which will gradually end too.- Martino gets up and gives Joana a kiss. She tries to dodge, but Martino grabs her tight and continues to kiss her.
- That's not how you'll be able to win me over!- Joana says, trying to push him away. Then Martino grabs her and manages to kiss her again, until Joana gives in.

Lying on the floor, looking at Martino, Joana saw Hevandrique's face caressing and kissing her.

- You will never like to be with a man, as you like to be with me.- Martino says, with the face of Hevandrique.

3

Joana, scared, woke up and saw that Hevandrique was beside her sleeping. A little scared, she ended up waking him up.

- What's going on?- He asks.
- Let's have sex.- Hevandrique looked at Joana, trying to understand what was going on with her. Joana put her hand inside Hevandrique's pants, who immediately withdrew her hand.
- This room is common and, at any time, Luís can come back.
- It doesn't matter.- Joana says, taking off her blouse, leaving only her bra on. Hevandrique got up and closed the curtain, picking up Joana's blouse and trying to put it back on.
- It's impossible here.- Says Hevandrique.
- Nothing is impossible.- Joana counters, also removing her bra.

- I brought a sandwich.- Luís says, opening the curtain and immediately finding Joana undressed. With that, Hevandrique irons her clothes, covering her. Luís closes the curtain again, leaving himself outside.

- Are you happy?- Shoots Hevandrique, also passing outside the curtain.

- Don't waste time, you guys!- Luís comments. Joana came out too and grabbed Hevandrique's hand, leading him away without saying a word.

- Where are we going?- Asks Hevandrique.

- Here.- Joana replies, sneaking into a bathroom.

- You know that if we're caught here, we're done, especially me, who's the director's nephew.

- I need you urgently.- Hevandrique looked at Joana's pleading face, leading her into one of the cabins. Joana took off her pants, followed by Hevandrique. In a mad attempt to balance themselves in such a cramped space, Joana had to put herself over the washstand, climbing onto Hevandrique's lap.

- I'm so tired. Me too.- Two nurses comment.- Hevandrique makes a sign of silence to Joana, putting her on the floor. Joana pushes Hevandrique so that he is sitting on the toilet, also giving him a sign of silence.

With a seductive smile, kneeling down, she begins to give an oral. Hevandrique puts his fingers between his teeth, not to moan, but it seemed almost impossible to contain himself, becoming more and more aroused. And the worst thing is that the nurses were on the other side, talking. Meanwhile Joana sits on Hevandrique's lap, tightening and loosening extremely. silent. When Joana reaches orgasm, she can't control a loud moan, hugging Hevandrique.

- Are you okay?- Asks one of the nurses, knocking on the door.

- Say yes.- Hevandrique whispers in Joana's ear, who was still experiencing her orgasm and didn't say a word.

- Is everything okay?- Repeats the nurse.

- Yes.- Hevandrique ends up answering, trying to imitate a female voice.

After a quarter of an hour in the bathroom, the nurses finally got tired of talking to each other and they managed to get out of the bathroom. Joana couldn't stop laughing.

- You know this isn't funny? - He says.

- Look who's talking, Mr. Humor, of course!- When they saw Marta in the hallway, both Hevandrique and Joana stopped to look at her. Marta also didn't react.- We need to talk.- Joana says to Marta.- Hevandrique says she's going to her cousin, leaving them to talk.

Marta stood still, waiting for Joana to speak, not knowing if the reason that made her want to talk to her was Hevandrique or Filipa.

- Sorry about today.- She ends up saying Joana.- Marta was more relieved to realize that Joana hadn't found out that António had attacked Hevandrique because of her, going to give her friend a hug, apologizing.

6

Joana and Marta entered the room and saw that Filipa had already woken up. She looked pale and scared. Joana looked at her and noticed that she had her pills. Her heart started to beat and she didn't know what to do, for sure Filipa would tell parents, thought Joana.

- Calm down, that's not what you're thinking.

- They're mine, I just asked your sister to keep them.

- I know they aren't.- Filipa says.- Yesterday, when I went out, I saw that box in your suitcase, but I wasn't curious to ask you what it was, and I've also seen you taking pills like that, exactly that color. You have HIV.- Accuses Filipa, looking contemptuously at her sister.- How many men have you slept with, to the point of contracting the disease?- Joana sat next to Filipa's bed, trying to touch her.

- Don't touch me.- Filipa says, looking at her sister with a disgusted face.

- What?

- You are a sinner, a vulgar one. How did you acquire this?

- Leave it alone. You went to a man's house in order to seduce him, not knowing if he has a disease or not!- Marta says, trying to put Filipa in her place.

- Does he have it too?- Filipa asks, scared.- Did you contaminate him?

- It was not me.

-Get out. Get out of here!- He starts screaming, not knowing what to do. Joana and Marta leave the room, before she gets into hysterics.

- My God, she's going to tell my parents! She will tell!- Joana says, panicking, starting to cry.

- Calm down.- Marta says, hugging her.- Calm down, friend.

After a few minutes, Filipa leaves the room, looking at her sister with the greatest of contempt. She asks Marta to leave them alone, signaling Joana to go back into the room.

- I want you to end everything with him.- Joana was speechless, wondering what the hell she was talking about.

- What?

- You're going to end up with Hevandrique.

- Why? That's none of your business.

- You know he has HIV, in case you want to stay with him, right?- Filipa went back to bed, lying down and closing her eyes.- Answer me, Filipa!- Then Filipa reopened her eyes and concentrated in Joan for some time. The sister also returned the look, not knowing what to say or how to react.

- After what happened yesterday, I don't want to know anything anymore. I can't keep him because of this damn disease, but neither will you. I prefer the two of us to be alone.- Joana was amazed at her sister's words, never thinking that she would ever get to this point.

- What kind of person are you? You had to be traumatized by what happened, but no, do you still have the courage and the strength to blackmail me?

You are the person who is always on the way to church, but who doesn't know how to forgive. You don't have any love for your neighbor, you're jealous, you're the worst kind of person that can exist in this world!

- Next week, the parents will return and I won't tell anything about what happened to me, and neither will you! So do what I tell you, before they have to abandon another daughter." Without remorse, without any weight of conscience, Filipa went back to bed. It seems that after what happened yesterday, her mean levels towards Joana have increased. Joana leaves the room without saying anything, closing the door. Marta looked at Joana and, by the look on her face, she knew that Filipa had not changed her mind. Really, she wanted her sister away from Hevandrique.

- She must have been weak and sensitive. How does a person who has just been through such a traumatic situation manage to remain so relaxed?

Brown eyes

Luís arrives and sees his cousin sitting with his back, sending a message on his cell phone, with a glass of water by his side. He sat down beside him, asking the waiter for a glass of beer.

- It's a pity you can't drink.- Luis says, trying to cheer him up, since Joana asked him for a break and António has never spoken to him since the argument at the hospital.- Here you are, trying to drown your tears with a glass of water. I bet you're texting Antonio. You are an amazing guy. Your girl dumps you and all you think about is talking to António. But what kind of relationship do you have?

- I can't believe you're still jealous of us!- Ironizes Hevandrique.

- Thank you.- Luís thanks the employee, who hands him the glass of beer. Takes a huge sip.- I was really thirsty.

- I bet so.- Says Hevandrique, concentrating on his cell phone. But Luís snatches the cell phone from his hand.- Give it back to me.- Demands Hevandrique, with a serious face. Luís reads the message and returns it, shaking his head, with a smile. - You're really crazy. I still hoped you were talking to her, but in the end it's always António.

- Joana just needs some time with her family. António is irritated with me.- He says, sighing.

A girl sat at the table opposite them. She was pretty pretty. With green eyes reflected in her brown skin and curly hair. It looked like a doll. The full lips. They could seduce any boy. Luís follows her with his eyes, unable to take a single moment away. When she decided to look up from her phone, she looked directly at their table, leaving Luís nervous and confused. And seeing that he was interested in the girl, Hevandrique smiled.

- You don't need to look away, just because she's looking at us.

- I bet she's looking at you.

- I know I'm prettier, but this time she's looking at you. It seems that, for the first time, a girl preferred your brown eyes to mine.- Hevandrique says, giving little shoves to his cousin, so that he would look at the girl.

- Stop it.- Hevadrique gets up and goes to her, making Luís even more nervous. After a few minutes, he comes back with a serious face and sits down, without saying a word. - Aren't you going to say anything?- Luis says, glancing at her, who was still around her cell phone.

- She's waiting for her boyfriend.- Luís sighs and takes a sip of his beer, disappointed.

- I'm kidding!- Hevandrique smiled.

- If you weren't sick, I'd kill you!

- Calm!

- She gave me the phone number and said I could give it to you.

- Seriously?

- Clear.

- But I didn't see you pointing at anything.

- You know my memory is a computer.

- If it didn't sound too sissy, I'd give you a kiss now.- Luis says, grinning from ear to ear.

Hevandrique grabbed his cousin's face and kissed him on the forehead. - Stop it, crazy! - says Luís, wiping his cousin's kiss and looking embarrassed at the girl, who, seeing the two, smiled.

Hugging the daughter

After two weeks, Hevandrique finally went to speak with Antonio. When she got to his office, he wasn't there. He sat in his friend's chair, looking around the office, all organized. That space was really the face of António, the most organized man on the face of the Earth. In order to be friends with him, he also had to become much more organized.

Hevandrique opens the computer and sees a photo of the two of them when they were still in college, at a time when they were both freshmen. The image made him smile and he saw that, even after the fight, António kept the photo of the two.

The friend enters the office and is startled to see Hevandrique. It closes the computer right away.

- Hi!- greets Hevandrique, getting up.

António sits on the sofa, sighing, while Hevandrique takes his place in the chair again, enjoying his friend, who said nothing.

- Marta and I agreed to go out.- António says. Hevandrique just looked at him, not knowing what to say. - Aren't you going to say anything?

- Good, I'm very happy.- António smiles. He looks at the ceiling, looks at his friend and looks back at the ceiling, displaying a sad face.

- She said that you didn't know anything and that it was something very fast, that even she didn't understand why, but that it wasn't a passion, just a superficial attraction that left her a little confused, so if you want to continue to be mine friend, try not to be alone with her again.- António says, with a serious air.

- I promise.- Answers Hevandrique, smiling.- António gets up and stretches out his arm, and Hevandrique goes to meet his friend, giving him a hug.

- I think this time I exaggerated, let me look at your face.- Antonio says, watching Hevandrique's face and slapping him afterwards.

- Oh! But I think the other time was much worse. At least now I didn't have to be hospitalized.

- You're much better now, I think I can give you another beating.- António jokes.

- One more beating from you, I can't take it. Just one more and I'll hire a bodyguard to walk with me.

-I'm sorry about that.- He says, hugging his friend.

- I think I deserved this life of being quite beautiful...- António gives Hevandrique a squeeze, who shouts for help, jokingly.

3

Suddenly, screams are heard and they immediately leave the office, trying to follow the sound of the screams. When Hevandrique sees Thiago, trying to free himself from one of the nurses.

- What happened?- Hevandrique asks, going to meet Thiago, who was crying desperately.

- They're going to shut down the machines today! The parents gave the authorization, but they can't do that!- Says Thiago, sitting on the floor, crying without control.

- Calm down.- Hevandrique says, giving him a hug.

- How did they do it? Please do something, please...

- What happened?- António asks one of the nurses.

- We are going to turn off the machines, the family gave their consent.

- The kid is very nervous and I bet the family isn't here, because they certainly don't want to watch their son's death. Why don't you do it later while we try to calm the kid down for now?

- All right, doctor.

- Please, doctor...- Thiago begs, approaching António, on his knees.- He hasn't even turned nineteen yet, he's only eighteen, how is it possible that he's going to die? Please don't let this happen.- António stared at Thiago, unable to answer him. Since the family has already signed, he could not do anything else, especially when the patient does not show any signs of improvement, as in the case of Tomás.- Please...- Hevandrique grabs Thiago, trying to lift him off the floor and help him. to sit.

- Calm down, the only solution will be to try to talk to his parents, we can't do anything more than that.

- But this is a crime, this is euthanasia! I never knew that, here in Portugal, that was legal, how can someone decide who lives and who dies? That's not fair, he might wake up.- Says Thiago, drowning in tears.

- The problem is that the chances are miniscule and, in the case of Tomás, medicine doesn't give any hope.

- Do you also think they have to turn off the machines?- He asks, looking at Hevandrique with the most painful face in the world.

- Look at your friend, imagine that, suddenly, he has an accident and the doctors say they have to turn off the machines, would you turn it off? Tell me, even if the chances are small!- António and Hevandrique looked at each other and put themselves in Thiago's shoes, managing to understand his suffering.

- Of course not. I want him to wake up too, but the only people who can save him are his parents, his family. They are the ones who have to go back on the decision and prevent the machines from being turned off.

- Will you accompany me to his house?- Hevandrique doesn't know how to respond.

- That's a little tricky.

- Please!- Seeing Thiago's distress, the only thing that Hevandrique could do was accompany him to Tomás's parents' house.

- You can go, I'll try to talk to the nurses so they don't turn off the machines now.

When they arrived, there were about twenty people in the room, some crying and others praying. The furniture was all leaning against the wall, so everyone could offer their condolences to his mother. They entered and saw a picture of Tomás smiling on the table and others scattered in every corner of the house.

- Come on, she must be in the office.- Thiago accompanied Hevandrique to the office, which was open, and you could hear Tomás' mother crying.

- Thiago?- She says, her eyes full of tears.

- Please Katia, I beg you, don't do this, don't turn off the machine. He is your only son and if I have hope, surely you must too... You are his mother, don't let him die like this, let him decide. If he's in a coma, it's because he's still trying to fight for his life.

Katia gets up and approaches Tomás, caressing his face and looking at him with pity. She knew that, in addition to her and her husband, the person who suffered the most from their son's situation was Thiago. Only he knew the pain she was going through.

- I wanted so much, but he doesn't give any hope, I'm sorry.

- Please!- Begs Thiago, already crying.- Let's wait at least another month, please, I can talk to my parents, they will accept to help you financially.

- Oh my dear... That's not the problem. The doctors talked to us and said he would never wake up again.

- Please, let's at least give him one more chance, please, I know you want it too, I want it, your husband wants it, he wants it too.- She says, pointing to Hevandrique.

- But by now, they must have turned off the machines.

- Not yet, I stopped them. Now you can go there and ask to cancel.- Katia shook her head and said yes. Thiago took a deep breath, giving Hevandrique a hug.

6

Joana had been at her parents' house for more than a month, gaining courage to tell them about her situation. She didn't want that, in an argument with Filipa, she ended up telling him. As much as she said she wouldn't, she couldn't just take her word for it, and she couldn't stay away from Hevandrique forever. This time without him was an eternity and she needed to see him again. She went to her parents' room, where her mother was combing her hair, getting ready to go to church. Her father, sitting organizing his suitcase. Joana entered, standing at the door, trying to gather the courage to speak to them.

- What is it, daughter? You have to prepare yourself, otherwise we'll be late.- Says the mother.

- I need to talk to you.- she says, leaning back, standing next to her mother. Her father looked at her, intimidating her, but Joana was determined. She took a deep breath, closed her eyes and confessed that she had HIV. The father's face hadn't changed, he continued to look at her the same way and said nothing. The mother's expression, on the other hand, changed completely, looking at her terrified daughter.- I know you will disown me.- She says, without holding back her tears.- I know that, perhaps, I will never look at her again. you, because I didn't follow the teachings you gave me, especially regarding virginity, but I couldn't hide it from you forever, I had to tell you. Forgive me.- The mother tried to speak, but the shock was such that she couldn't. Finally, the father changed his expression, showing a terrified face. - Aren't you going to say anything?

- How did that happen?- Asks the father.

- Because of a boy. I didn't know he was infected and he transmitted the disease to me, only later did I find out, when he became extremely ill.- The father massaged his face, not knowing what to say. The mother, on the other hand, got up and hugged Joana.

- I'm sorry, daughter, I'm sorry you have to face this alone.

- Drop her! - Says the father, getting up, nervous. And leaving both Mafalda and Joana scared.- Are you happy now? Well, I didn't want you to leave the house. I knew that this world was cruel enough for you to face it alone.- Says Rui, crying.- Please leave.

- I knew this would happen, just as you pushed my brother away, you will do the same to me. You are a pastor, but you judge yourself to be Jesus Christ, with the right to judge the whole world.

- Don't talk to me like that! - shouts Rui, standing up towards Joana, leaving her scared, while Mafalda cried.

- How do you want me to react, knowing that my daughter, that my girl, has this disease? How? Tell me! I'm not going to push you away, your brother left, because he preferred drugs over us, I never abandoned him, now how can you, my daughter...- Rui kneels down, crying, with a desolate heart . Joana also kneels down, giving her father a hug.

- I'm so sorry, Dad. I'm very sorry, forgive me for this.

- I just wanted my children to be happy, but it seems that I acted badly when it came to educating you.- He says, hugging his daughter.

- You gave us the best education in the world, It's just that the world itself is cruel, it's not your fault, I'm sorry, Dad.

A kiss on the forehead

Joana wanted to run into Hevandrique's arms, but first she needed to close a chapter in her story, which was still open. She went to the hospital where she last saw Martino, and where she first learned that she had HIV. The last time she saw him, Martino had a high fever and a lung infection, which left him weak and unable to breathe independently.

Upon entering the hospital, my heart ached. It was a hospital that brought back very sad memories.

Things she somehow wanted to forget, but after her parents' forgiveness, she needed to talk to him before it was too late. Joana didn't know if he was still there. He could have only stayed for a while and left shortly after, but she wanted to find Martino and the only lead she had was that hospital.

3

Joana sat down for a few moments, to gain strength, so that she could ask about Martino. He could be dead, and that was one thing that scared her a lot. As much as Martino had done something terrible to her, he no longer wished him dead and wanted, if he wasn't in that hospital bed, that he would at least be in good health, having stopped living contaminating women in clubs.

- Very good afternoon, I wanted to talk to the patient Martino Ferreira da Silvava.- The nurse looked at the list of patients and said that she could go up to room 300. Even the number was scary. Joana's heart was beating wildly. Seeing Martino's room number, she stood outside for some time without daring to enter. She knew she needed to get inside, but she was quite afraid of what she might find on the other side. It was a very hidden ward and seemed to be for the terminally ill.

- Good afternoon.- Says a nurse, entering the room. Joana, in a strange way and with sweat on her face, took a step forward and entered Martino's room. She got tears in her eyes to see him in that state. She hadn't seen him in over a year and she never thought he could be like this. Joana approached him and he was sleeping. The wrinkled skin, pale and thin, had black spots all over her body. His bones were all in sight, he was so thin. Joan cried. Until then, she still had a faint hope that she would be told that Martino was no longer in the hospital. She'd already forgiven him, in a way, but seeing him in that state, sick and helpless, in a diaper, didn't even seem like the wonderful man who had charmed her. Joana took his hand and he woke up. When he saw Joana, he smiled, leaving her with a heavy heart and shedding even more tears.

- Hello.- He greets him, his strength failing, but always smiling. He wasn't much for smiles, but at that moment, he couldn't stop smiling.

Since he opened his eyes and saw Joana, he put a smile on his lips, which he never took away, even seeing Joana in tears.

- Hello.- Joana reciprocates, trying not to cry like a baby.

- I'm sorry, but I can't sit down to talk to you.- He says, with a tired voice. He seemed to be making a huge effort to talk.

- It doesn't matter.- Joana says, sitting on a chair that was there, next to the bed.

- I thought I'd never see you again, I'm glad you came. Thank you so much for coming, I knew this would happen.

- Of course I do.- Joana says, looking at him with pity and a heavy heart. In that moment, she didn't feel an iota of hatred or resentment for him, only pity. Such a pity, she could only cry.

- I wanted to apologize. Not just you, but all the girls I infected too. I was a monster, I did the worst thing a human being can do, and now I'm paying for it all. I know there's no justification for this, but I hated all women, and all because of a woman, who has nothing to do with you.- Martino took a deep breath, with some difficulty.- My mother used drugs. When my father left her, she got worse. My father took me and my brothers to live with him. When I was fifteen, I always liked to visit my mother, I didn't like to leave her alone. One day, my father took us to her house, we slept there and she infected us with the virus, introducing her blood with a needle into our veins, committing suicide right away, with a shot in the head. She left a note for my father, saying, I hope you have a good life. My father was desperate to learn that his three children were contaminated. My 6 year old brother died a year later and the other died three years later. My father started drinking heavily, becoming an alcoholic. Our lives were destroyed because of that woman I called mother. That I loved and cried. When she died. After some time, my father also committed suicide, leaving a letter apologizing to me for leaving me alone. That left me so, but so frustrated, that I decided to take revenge on all women. I can't say for sure how many people I infected, but I can say that there were many, at least twenty women, who may have also infected other people. I would date several women, make them trust me, and when I managed to infect them, I would disappear from their lives without giving a single explanation. That's how I lived my life, hurting all the women I got involved with, so don't cry, because it will make me even sadder, because I don't deserve your tears, since God gave me the my last wish to be able to apologize to you and, above all, for you to be well.- Then Martino turned around, looking at Joana, who was crying profusely.

6

- Right now, I'm living the last days of my life. I can only regret everything I've done. I haven't been able to contact any of them because I've been cooped up in this hospital for the past year. My situation got a lot worse, because I stopped taking care of myself, I have several diseases in my body, the doctors don't give me hope to live a new day and they are always surprised when they enter this room and I'm still alive. This means that at any moment I can die, but I think I'm still alive because God gave me a chance to apologize to at least one of you.

- I'm very sorry.- Joana says, taking Martino's hand.

- It's so good to feel your touch once again.- He says, once again, smiling.- It may seem like a lie, but you were the woman I liked the most. You were the woman I stayed with the longest, even after I infected you, and you were the only one I regretted. Even at that time, I know it's difficult, but I hope you have a good life, that you can find someone and that you don't suffer any prejudice.- Martino says, his eyes brimming with tears.

- I have a good life. I met a good guy, who also has the disease, but we live as if we don't. We are a normal couple, who like to go out and be with friends. As they say, there are good things for the bad and bad things for the good. Maybe if I didn't get the disease, I'd never meet him. That's why I sometimes say that I'm happy having this disease. So I forgive you for having infected me, and I hope you can forgive yourself too. I know I can't forgive you for other women, but deep down, we should take better care of ourselves too. And I also hope they are all well. I know they are.- Joana says, squeezing her hand again and crying like a child.

Martino smiled, as if saying goodbye. Her eyes filled with tears once more and he closed them, as if he were sleeping. Joana knew he was dead. She stared at him desolately, not knowing what to do. One of the nurses noticed and called a doctor, who confirmed what Joana was already expecting. Martino had passed away.

Joana couldn't stand it and cried so much, her chest felt like it could burst from so much suffering. She didn't even know why she cried so much for a man who had done her so much harm, but she had such pity, she couldn't explain. She suffered, but there are people who suffered more than she did, and sure enough, those people were Hevandrique and Martino.

Joana showed up at Hevandrique's house quite desolate, still crying and soaking wet from the rain. Hevandrique gave her a hug and picked her up, carrying her to the bed, covering her with several sheets to keep her warm, turning on the heater.

- What is it? - Joana could barely speak through her tears, and Hevandrique couldn't understand what had happened.

- I went to see Martino, the man who infected me. I never thought that watching him die... would make me so bad.- He ends up counting, between sobs.- I thought I suffered, but, in fact, you and he suffered much more than I did. I always had people to support me, but he didn't. He grew up alone and it was his mother who infected him, out of hatred for his father. How can a mother do so much evil to her own child? I love you, please don't ever do anything crazy because of this disease.

- I promise.- whispers Hevandrique.

9

Martino was buried and only Joana, Hevandrique, Marta, António and Luís were present. No one else showed up for the farewell and they couldn't find any of his family members. If Joana hadn't found him the moment she found him, only the doctors, a nurse and the priest would be there. And nobody else. Even one of the nurses said that during this year he's been hospitalized, he hasn't had a single visit. Not a friend, not a family member, not a girlfriend. What killed him was loneliness. Of course, it was already difficult for him to overcome the disease when he was admitted to the hospital, but it was possible. He just couldn't get over the illness because of the guilt and loneliness he felt. And Joana couldn't stand it, she was crying so much. She never thought she would cry so much out of pity for someone and just thought that this could happen to her too, if she didn't have her family, Hevandrique or Marta. The same could happen to Hevandrique as well, and that terrified her.

- Where is your girlfriend?- Asks Luís.

- What did you come here to do?- Hevandrique asks.

- Maybe because of the guilt of having done that with her sister, I don't know, I can't explain it either.- Hevandrique smiled, looking at his cousin.- Joana?

- She wanted to spend some time alone with him.

- This is going to seem a little insensitive, but aren't you a little jealous of him? It's okay that he's been through a lot, but seeing my girl cry for another like this isn't a very pleasant thing to see.

- I would be jealous if I were António, crying for another friend like that.- Hevandrique jokes.

- Do you know they've legalized gay marriage? I don't know why you guys keep hiding.

- He says he prefers to have me as a lover.

- I think we better finish this conversation.- Finishes Luís, lighting a cigarette. António took Luis' cigarette and put it out on the floor with the toe of his shoe.

- You know this is bad for him and yet you still smoke.

- There's your boyfriend trying to protect you.

Joana returned, walking slowly, until she reached the group, holding hands with Hevandrique, who kissed her forehead.

- Shall we go?- Asks Hevandrique.

-Of course.- Joana says, smiling for the first time in two days.- Joana realized that HIV is a disease that everyone fears and hates, but even so, she is happier with it than when she didn't have it. Amazingly, after telling her parents, they grew closer to her and built a more beautiful relationship. For the first time, the father talked about looking for her brother, because, in a strange way, he also noticed that if he doesn't support his children in the disease, things can still get worse and Rui was willing to get his son back.

The wedding

Joan was nervous. Not just because she was going to go down the aisle, but also because her fiancé hadn't arrived yet and she was ready. She had decided that she would not be late for a single minute. But it seems that Hevandrique decided otherwise.

- Calm down, he will arrive.- Marta says, trying to calm her down.

- I'll kill that bastard. Why didn't he tell me he didn't want a house?" Joana snapped, already angry and her nerves on edge.

- You look very beautiful.- Luis praises, leaning on the car door.

- Where's your cousin? - Joana asks, already unable to hide her nervousness.

- I warned you that he prefers António, I think they ran away together, because neither of them is at the altar. Neither the godfather nor the groom.- Joana shoots Luís a glare and he leaves without saying anything else.

- Try calling António.- Joana says to her friend.

- I've tried, but he doesn't answer and Hevandrique's number is disconnected.- Arthur, Joana's brother, left already distressed, asking his sister for her fiancé.

- I'm also trying to get in touch with him.- Joana says.- If he doesn't show up, don't worry. I haven't been in the army all this time for nothing, I'll finish him off.

- Only you! When everyone thought they would find you in a rehabilitation clinic, after all you were in the army.- Says Marta.

- It's not the time for you to admire him, it's time for my fiancé and his best man to show up.

- Didn't they really run away together?

- For!

- Sorry, I just wanted to break the ice.- Marta says.

- The groom has arrived.- Announces Mafalda.- Joana took a deep breath. After an hour of suffocation, Hevandrique appeared. From perspiring so much, Joana no longer had her make-up on, not even her veil, which she tore off with nervousness. At that moment, Joana didn't even think about putting the veil back on. She called her father and went up to the altar. Worse than her, only the groom, who showed up in his hospital clothes, looking like he was going to work, but at that moment, Joana just wanted to marry the man she loved. She went to meet him and gave him a tight hug.

    - I thought you would be late, normally, brides are late!

    - By the way, where were you?- Joana asks, already in the middle of the altar.

    - Isn't it better if we get married first?

    - Tomás woke up from his coma today and, I don't know why, but he really wanted to see you get married.- António says.

Joana looks back and sees Tomás sitting in a wheelchair next to Thiago. Tears came to her eyes. She can't even believe he was alive and it seems she wasn't the only one happy in that church, everyone was happy, even people who thought they would never be happy again. At that moment, at least at that moment, everyone had a smile on their lips. Joana and Hevandrique for the wedding, Thiago because his great friend woke up. Joana's parents because their son is back and their daughter is getting married. All the members of the HIV group were there, also happy, with their families. After seeing this vision of happiness, Joana could only turn around and kneel so that the priest would marry her to Hevandrique.

ANAMNESIS OF YOU

JANDIRA KAPAPELO

ANAMNESIS OF YOU